"The sheriff doesn't b

Rand moved in beside her and put his hand on her shoulder. "I believe you."

She couldn't look at him. His voice was so gentle, and she knew she would see the same tenderness in his eyes and she would lose it. She would collapse into a puddle of tears and ugly cry all over him. "I feel like I'm waiting for something to happen," she said. "Something bad."

"You believe they're still here," Rand said.

"They've been pursuing me for fifteen years," she said. "Why leave when they've gotten this close?"

He nodded. He wanted to put his arm around her and try to comfort her, but he wasn't sure she would be receptive. "What can I do?" he asked instead.

She pressed her lips together, arms crossed, shoulders hunched. Then she raised her eyes to his. "Tell me about your sister," she said.

MOUNTAIN CAPTIVE

CINDI MYERS

Harlequin

INTRIGUE

**Harlequin®
INTRIGUE™**

ISBN-13: 978-1-335-45716-5

Mountain Captive

Copyright © 2025 by Cynthia Myers

Harlequin Enterprises ULC
22 Adelaide St. West, 41st Floor
Toronto, Ontario M5H 4E3, Canada
www.Harlequin.com

Printed in Lithuania

Cindi Myers is the author of more than seventy-five novels. When she's not plotting new romance storylines, she enjoys skiing, gardening, cooking, crafting and daydreaming. A lover of small-town life, she lives with her husband and two spoiled dogs in the Colorado mountains.

Books by Cindi Myers

Harlequin Intrigue

Eagle Mountain: Criminal History

Mile High Mystery
Colorado Kidnapping
Twin Jeopardy
Mountain Captive

Eagle Mountain: Critical Response

Deception at Dixon Pass
Pursuit at Panther Point
Killer on Kestrel Trail
Secrets of Silverpeak Mine

Eagle Mountain Search and Rescue

Eagle Mountain Cliffhanger
Canyon Kidnapping
Mountain Terror
Close Call in Colorado

Visit the Author Profile page at Harlequin.com.

CAST OF CHARACTERS

Dr. Rand Martin—Army veteran and trauma surgeon Rand Martin joins search and rescue to become more involved in his new community.

Chris Mercer—Search and rescue volunteer Chris Mercer has a reputation for being dedicated, artistically talented and standoffish. But the arrival of a new group of campers in the area reveals the dark secrets of Chris's past.

Edmund Harrison—The charismatic leader of a group called the Vine, Harrison goes by the title of "the Exalted" and claimed Chris as his own when she was only nine. He has come to Eagle Mountain to claim her.

Jedediah—The Exalted's right-hand man makes sure everyone follows their leader's commands, and he's determined to bring Chris back into the fold.

Serena Rogers—Born into the Vine, ten-year-old Serena, now an orphan, has been selected as the Exalted's next young bride.

Harley—The Rhodesian ridgeback is Chris's protector and best friend.

Chapter One

Rand Martin had built his reputation on noticing details—the tiny nick in an artery that was the source of life-threatening blood loss; the almost microscopic bit of shrapnel that might lead to a deadly infection; the panic in a wounded man's eyes that could send his vitals out of control; the tremor in a fellow surgeon's hand that meant he wasn't fit to operate. As a trauma surgeon—first in the military, then in civilian life—Rand noticed the little things others overlooked. It made him a better doctor, and it equipped him to deal with the people in his life.

But sometimes that focus on the small picture got in the way of his big-picture job. Today, his first call as medical adviser for Eagle Mountain Search and Rescue, he was supposed to be focusing on the sixty-something man sprawled on the side of a high mountain trail. But Rand's attention kept shifting to the woman who knelt beside the man. Her blue-and-yellow vest identified her as a member of the search and rescue team, but her turquoise hair and full sleeve of colorful tattoos set her apart from the other volunteers. That, and the wariness that radiated off her as she surveyed the crowd that was fast gathering around her and her patient on the popular hiking trail.

"Everyone move back and give us some space," Rand

ordered, and, like the men and women he had commanded in his mobile surgical unit in Kabul, the crowd obeyed and fell back.

SAR Captain Danny Irwin rose from where he had been crouched on the patient's other side and greeted Rand. "Thanks for coming out," he said.

"Are you the doctor?" Another woman, blond hair in a ponytail that streamed down her back, rushed forward.

"Dr. Rand Martin." He didn't offer his hand, already pulling on latex gloves, ready to examine his patient. The blue-haired woman had risen also, and was edging to one side of the trail. As if she was trying to blend in with the crowd—a notion Rand found curious. Nothing about this woman would allow her to blend in. Even without the wildly colored hair and the ink down her arm, she was too striking to ever be invisible.

"My dad has a heart condition," the blonde said. "I tried to tell him he shouldn't be hiking at this altitude, but he wouldn't listen, and now this has happened."

"Margo, please!" This, from the man on the ground. He had propped himself up on his elbows and was frowning at the woman, presumably his daughter. "I hurt my leg. It has nothing to do with my heart."

"You don't know that," she said. "Maybe you fell because you were lightheaded or had an irregular heartbeat. If you weren't so stubborn—"

A balding man close to the woman's age moved up and put his hands on the woman's shoulders. "Let's wait and see what the doctor has to say," he said, and led Margo a few feet away.

Rand crouched beside the man. He was pale, sweating and breathing hard. Not that unusual, considering the bone sticking out of his lower leg. He was probably in a lot of pain from that compound fracture, and despite his protestation that nothing was wrong with his heart, the pain and shock could aggravate an existing cardiac condition. "What happened?" Rand asked.

"We were coming down the trail and Buddy fell." This, from another woman, with short gray curls. She sat a few feet away, flanked by two boys—early- or preteens, Rand guessed. The boys were staring at the man on the ground, freckles standing out against their pale skin.

"I stepped on a rock, and it rolled," Buddy offered. "I heard a snap." He grimaced. "Hurts like the devil."

"We'll get you something for the pain." Rand saw that someone—Danny or the blue-haired woman—had already started an intravenous line. "Do you have a medical history?" he asked Danny.

The SAR captain—an RN in his day job—handed over a small clipboard. Buddy was apparently sixty-seven, on a couple of common cardiac drugs. No history of medication allergies, though Rand questioned him again to be absolutely sure. Then he checked the clipboard once more. "Mr. Morrison, we're going to give you some morphine for the pain. It should take effect within a few minutes. Then we're going to splint your leg, pack it in ice to keep the swelling down, and get you down the mountain and to the hospital for X-rays and treatment."

"But his heart!" Margo, who'd shoved away from the balding man—her husband, perhaps—rushed forward again.

"Are you experiencing any chest pain?" Rand asked, even as he pulled out a stethoscope. "Palpitations?"

"No." Buddy glanced toward his daughter and lowered

his voice, his tone confiding. "I had a quadruple bypass nine months ago. I completed cardiac rehab, and I'm just fine. Despite what my daughter would have you believe, I'm not an idiot. My doctor thought this vacation was a fine idea. I'm under no activity restrictions."

"Your doctor probably has no idea you would decide to hike six miles at ten thousand feet," Margo said.

Rand slid the stethoscope beneath Buddy Morrison's T-shirt and listened to the strong, if somewhat rapid, heartbeat. He studied the man's pupils, which were fine. Some of the color was returning to his cheeks. Rand moved to check the pulse in his leg below the break.

"Chris, come hold this," Danny called over to the young blue-haired woman after he had hooked the man's IV line to a bag of saline. She held it, elevated, while he injected the morphine into the line. Rand watched her while trying to appear not to. Up close, she had fine lines at the corners of her eyes, which were a chocolatey brown, fringed with heavily mascaraed lashes. She had a round face, with a slight point to her chin and a Cupid's bow mouth with a slightly fuller lower lip. It was a strikingly beautiful face, with a mouth he would have liked to kiss.

He pushed the inappropriate thought away and focused on working with Danny to straighten the man's leg. Buddy groaned as the broken tip of the bone slid back under the skin, and the gray-haired woman let out a small cry as well. Margo took a step toward them. "What are you doing?" she asked. "You're hurting him!"

"He'll feel a lot better when the bones of the leg are in line and stabilized," Rand said, and began to fit the inflatable splint around the man's leg. Once air was added, the splint would form a tight, formfitting wrap that would make for a much more comfortable trip down the mountain on the litter.

The splint in place, Rand stood and stepped back. "You can take it from here," he told Danny, and watched as half a dozen more volunteers swarmed in to assemble a wheeled litter, transferred Buddy onto it, and secured him, complete with a crash helmet, ice packs around his leg and warm blankets over the rest of his body.

While they worked, another female volunteer explained to Buddy's family what would happen next. In addition to the family and the search and rescue volunteers, a crowd of maybe a dozen people clogged the trail, so each new hiker who descended the route was forced to join the bottleneck and wait. The onlookers talked among themselves, and more than a few snapped photographs.

Danny moved to Rand's side. "It's a little different from assessing a patient at the hospital ER," Danny said.

"Different from the battlefield too," Rand said. There was no scent of mortar rounds and burning structures here, and no overpowering disinfectant scent of a hospital setting. Only sunshine and a warm breeze with the vanilla-tinged scent of ponderosa pine.

"Thanks for coming out," Danny said again.

"You could have handled it fine without me," Rand said. He had heard enough from people around town to know Eagle Mountain SAR was considered one of the top wilderness-response teams in the state.

"The family calmed down a lot when I assured them we had a 'real doctor' on the way to take care of their father," Danny said. He glanced over to where Margo and her mother were huddled with the balding man and the two boys, their anxious faces focused on the process of loading

Buddy into the litter. "But I won't call you except in cases of emergency, if that's what you want."

"No. I want you to treat me like any other volunteer," Rand said.

"You mean, go through the training, attend the meetings, stuff like that?"

"Yes. That's exactly what I mean. I like being outdoors, and I need to get out of the office and the operating room. I'm in good physical shape, so I think I could be an asset to the team, beyond my medical knowledge."

"That's terrific," Danny said. "We'd be happy to have you. If you have time, come back to headquarters with us, and I'll introduce you around. Or come to the next regular meeting. Most of the volunteers will be there. I'll give you a training schedule and a bunch of paperwork to sign."

"Sounds good." Rand turned back to the crowd around the litter as it began to move forward. He searched among the dozen or so volunteers for the woman with the blue hair but didn't see her. Then he spotted her to one side. She stood in the shadow of a pine, staring up the trail.

He followed her gaze, trying to determine what had caught her attention. Then he spotted the man—midforties, a dirty yellow ball cap covering his hair and hiding his eyes. But he was definitely focused on the woman, his posture rigid.

Rand looked back toward the blue-haired woman, but she was gone. She wasn't by the tree. She wasn't with the volunteers or in the crowd of onlookers that was now making its way down the trail.

"Is something wrong?" Danny asked.

"The volunteer who was with Mr. Morrison when I arrived," he said. "With the blue hair."

"Chris. Chris Mercer."

"Has she been a volunteer long?"

"Off and on for four years. Her work has taken her away a couple of times—she's an artist. But she always comes back to the group." Danny looked around. "I don't see her now."

"She was just here," Rand said. "I was wondering where she went."

"There's no telling with Chris. She's a little unconventional but a good volunteer. She told me she was hiking about a mile down the trail when the call went out, so she was first on the scene," Danny said. "She's supposed to stick around for report back at the station. Maybe she's already headed back there."

"Looks like she left something behind," Rand said. He made his way to the spot where she had been standing and picked up a blue day pack, the nylon outer shell faded and scuffed. He unzipped the outer pocket and took out a business card. "'Chris Mercer, Aspen Leaf Gallery,'" he read.

"That's Chris's," Danny said. He held out his hand. "I'll put it in the lost and found bin at headquarters."

"That's okay. I'll take it to her." Rand slipped one strap of the pack over his shoulder.

"Suit yourself," Danny said. He and Rand fell into step behind the group wheeling the litter. Morrison's family was hiking ahead, though the daughter, Margo, kept looking back to check on their progress. Every twenty minutes or so, the volunteers switched positions, supporting the litter and guiding it down the trail or walking alongside it with the IV bag suspended. They continually checked on Mr. Morrison, asking him how he was doing, assessing his condition, staying alert for any change that might indicate something they had missed. Something going wrong.

Rand felt the tension in his own body, even as he reminded himself that this was a simple accident—a fall that had resulted in a fracture, free of the kinds of complications that had plagued his patients on the battlefield, and the motor vehicle collision and gunshot victims he often met in the emergency room where he now worked.

Heavy footfalls on the trail behind them made Rand turn, in time to see the man in the dirty yellow ball cap barreling toward them. The man brushed against Rand as he hurried by, head down, boots raising small puffs of dirt with each forceful step. "Hey!" Rand called out, prepared to tell the man to be more careful. But the guy broke into a run and soon disappeared down the trail.

"Guess he had somewhere he needed to be," Danny said.

"Guess so," Rand said, but the hair on the back of his neck rose as he remembered the expression on Chris's face as she had stared at the man.

She hadn't merely been curious or even afraid of the man.

She had been terrified.

Chapter Two

Chris prowled the bedroom of her apartment above the art gallery, throwing random items into the suitcase on her bed, her mother's voice on the phone trying, but failing, to soothe her jangled nerves. "I'm sure the man was only looking at you because you're so striking," April Mercer said.

Chris stepped over her dog, Harley, who raised his head and looked at her with brown eyes full of concern. The Rhodesian ridgeback mix had picked up on her mood as soon as she entered the apartment, and he refused to be more than a few inches away from her. "I don't think so," Chris told her mother. "He looked familiar. Do you remember that guy who used to stand at the back of the room, glaring at everyone during Sunday-night meetings? Jedediah?" Chris grabbed a handful of socks and stuffed them into the side of the suitcase. A shudder went through her as she remembered the man on the trail.

"Oh, honey, I'm sure it wasn't him," April said. "It's been so long. I'm sure all of those people have forgotten about you by now."

"Do you really believe that, Mom?"

Her mother's silence was all the answer she needed. Jedediah and the others hadn't forgotten about Chris. That hadn't been her name back them, but that wouldn't matter to them.

"Would you really remember what he looked like after all these years?" April asked finally.

It wasn't the man's features that had been so familiar to her, but the look in his eyes. So full of hate. "He sure acted as if he recognized me."

"How could he?" April asked. "You changed your hair and had that nose job. And you were twelve years old. You were a child when he saw you last."

"I know." She swallowed down the rising panic and forced herself to stop and breathe deeply. "I just… The way he looked at me."

Harley stood and leaned against her. She bent and rubbed behind the dog's ears, finding solace in his solid presence.

"He's just a creep," April said. "There are plenty of them out there. If you really think he's a threat, tell the sheriff. Didn't you tell me he's a decent guy?"

"Yes. I mean, I've only interacted with Sheriff Walker on search and rescue missions, but he has a good reputation." Still, how would he react if she told him someone she had last seen when she was twelve had been glaring at her? And did she really want to reveal that whole sordid story to anyone here?

"You know you're always welcome to stay with me for a while if it makes you feel better," April said.

"I know." But Chris had already hidden out at her mom's place three times in the past two years. And at least one of those times had been a false alarm. She had heard the talk from other search and rescue members about how often she was out of town. Everyone seemed understanding, but that was probably because they thought her work as an artist was taking her away for weeks or months at a time. "I'm tired of running away," she said.

"Oh, honey."

The tenderness in April's voice might have broken a weaker woman. But Chris had had years to develop a hard shell around her emotions. "I was just wondering if you had heard anything about Jedediah. If you knew if he had a reason to be in this area."

"No," April said. "I try to keep tabs on people, but I have to rely on the few friendly contacts I still have, and they're understandably reluctant to reveal too much. But Colorado and Jedediah have never come up in our conversations."

Chris nodded, even though she knew her mother couldn't see her. "Okay, that's good. I guess."

"I'm sorry this happened to upset you," her mother said. "But I don't think it has anything to do with what happened all those years ago."

"You're right." Chris let go of the dog and turned to stare at the suitcase, into which she had apparently packed a dozen T-shirts and eight pairs of socks but no underwear or pants. "I'll just…keep my eyes open, and if I see anyone suspicious or threatening, I'll tell the sheriff."

"That sounds like a good plan," April said. "But know you can come stay with me anytime."

A knock on the door set her heart racing. Was it Jedediah? Had he managed to find her? "I have to go now, Mom."

"I love you," April said.

Harley was already moving toward the door. He hadn't barked or even growled, but the ridge of hair along his spine stood at attention.

"I love you too," Chris whispered. She slid the phone into

her pocket and tiptoed toward the door, careful not to make a sound. Holding her breath, she peered through the peephole with Harley pressed against her side, his body taut.

Chris exhaled in a rush as she recognized the man on the other side. She unfastened the security chain and dead bolt and eased the door open a scant two inches. "Hello?"

"Chris Mercer?" The doctor who was now working with search and rescue asked. She couldn't remember his name, but she wasn't likely to forget his face anytime soon. Blue eyes, curly dark hair, cleft chin—he had definitely made her look twice when she had first seen him.

"What do you want?" she asked.

He held up her day pack. "You left this behind on the trail. I thought you'd want it back."

"How did you find me?" She didn't like the idea that a stranger—no matter how good looking or well intentioned—could walk right up to her front door.

"There's a card for the gallery downstairs in the outside pocket of the pack," he said. "I asked and the woman at the register told me you were upstairs."

Chris frowned. She would have to have a talk with Jasmine. "Thanks." She opened the door wider and reached for the pack. Thoughtless of her to have left it, but that showed how shaken up she had been.

Harley shoved forward and stuck his head out the door. He glared at the doctor, a low rumble vibrating the air.

The doctor took a step back. "Hello, there," he addressed the dog.

"That's Harley. He won't hurt you." Not unless she told him to. The dog was trained to protect, though most of the time he was a genuine sweetheart. "Just hand me the pack."

The doctor—why couldn't she remember his name?—held it out of reach. "Are you okay?" he asked.

"I'm fine. Can I have my pack, please?"

He handed it over. "You left the trail in a hurry," he said. "We didn't get a chance to meet. I'm Rand Martin."

"Thanks for returning my pack, Rand." She tried to close the door, but he caught the frame and held it.

Harley's growl intensified, his body rigid. Rand glanced down at him but held his ground. "First, I want to make sure you're okay," he said. "You looked really upset back there on the trail. You still look upset."

"I'm fine."

"Who was the man watching you?"

Her breath caught. "You saw him too?"

"Yes."

"Do you know him?" she asked.

"Why don't I come in, and we'll talk about it?"

Just then, Jasmine, a petite woman with short red hair and white-rimmed glasses, appeared at the top of the stairs at the end of the hall. "Is everything okay, Chris?" she asked. Her gaze shifted to Rand, then back to Chris, eyes bright with curiosity.

"Everything is fine." Chris signaled for Harley to stand down and opened the door a little wider. "Come on in," she said to Rand. At least if he turned out to be a threat, Jasmine would be able to identify him. Not that there was anything particularly threatening about the doctor. He was older than Chris—early forties, maybe—but he was fit and strong. He exuded calm, and he struck her as someone who would be good to have on her side should Jedediah, or whoever that man had been, decide to show up.

He moved into her apartment, and she shut the door behind him. Harley stayed between them, silent but wary. Rand stopped in front of a painting beside the front door, an eight-by-ten canvas depicting a young girl crouched beside a pool in a mountain stream. A face was reflected in the water—a much older woman meant to represent the girl in her later years. "One of yours?" Rand asked.

"Yes." She dropped the pack onto the floor beside the sofa. "Do you know the man who was watching me there on the trail?"

He shook his head. "No. But you looked like you recognized him."

"I thought I did, but I was wrong."

"Then why were you afraid?"

"I wasn't afraid." The lie came easily. She was practiced at hiding that part of herself.

"You were terrified." He spoke with such certainty, as if he knew her and her innermost thoughts. But he wasn't saying the words to use her emotions against her as a weapon. If anything, his expression telegraphed understanding. As if he, too, had felt terror before and knew its paralyzing power.

She turned away from him. "I'm a single woman," she said. "I don't appreciate when a man I don't know takes such an intense interest in me." Would Rand take the hint that he, himself, should leave her alone?

"For what it's worth, I looked for him on the way down the trail, but I didn't see him again." He looked around her place. "I take it he didn't follow you here?"

She shook her head. She had made sure she was alone before she risked coming here. "Thanks for returning my pack," she said. "I really have things to do now." Unpack her suitcase, for one. Maybe do a little research online and try to find out what happened to Jedediah. Could she dredge up his last name from memory? Had she ever known it?

"Would you have dinner with me?"

The question startled her so much her mouth dropped open. She stared. Rand stared back, his lips tipped up at one corner, blue eyes full of amusement. Was he laughing at her? "What did you say?" she asked.

"Would you have dinner with me?"

"No." Absolutely not.

"Why not?"

"I don't date."

"Why not?"

"I just… I'm not interested in a relationship."

"Neither am I," he said.

"Why not?" She hadn't meant to say the words out loud, but seriously, the man was gorgeous. A doctor. He appeared to have a decent personality.

"I'm a trauma surgeon. I have a terrible schedule. I can't even get a dog, my hours are so unpredictable. Any woman in my life invariably ends up feeling neglected and resenting me."

"Then why ask me out? I don't do one-night stands either."

That little barb didn't faze him. "Everyone can use a friend," he said gently.

She hugged her arms across her chest. "You don't want to be friends with me."

"Why not?"

"I come with a lot of baggage."

He laughed. A loud, hearty guffaw. The sound elicited a sharp rebuke from Harley.

"It's okay," Rand said to the dog. He crouched and offered his hand for the dog to sniff. Harley approached cautiously, then allowed Rand to pet his sleek side.

Chris glared at him. "What's so funny?"

"Show me a person over twenty who doesn't have baggage, and I'll show you someone not worth knowing," he said. "Come on. Have a burger and a beer with me."

The offer tempted her, if only for the chance to have an evening outside her own head. She took a step back. "No. I think you need to leave now."

She expected him to argue, to turn charming or pleading. Instead, he only stood and took a card from his wallet and offered it to her.

She stared at it but didn't take it. He laid it on the table beside the sofa. "That's my number, if you need anything." He shrugged. "In case that guy shows up, for instance."

"What are you going to do if he does?"

"I could probably persuade him to leave you alone."

From anyone else, the words might have come across as a brag. From Rand, they rang true. He wasn't an overly big man, but he had a wiry strength, and the attitude of someone who wouldn't back down from a fight. "Thanks," she said. "But I'll be fine."

He nodded and left, letting himself out and shutting the door softly behind him. She locked up, then leaned against the paneled surface of the door. If Rand could find her so easily, Jedediah could too. The thought ought to have renewed the terror she'd felt earlier, but instead, the idea annoyed her. She had told her mother the truth when she said she was tired of running away. Jedediah had been powerful and threatening when she had known him before, capable of hurting her. But she wasn't a child anymore. And she knew the truth behind the lies he and others had told. She didn't have to keep running. She could stay and resist.

This time, she might even win.

Chapter Three

The parking lot at Eagle Mountain Search and Rescue head-quarters was full by the time Rand pulled in Thursday evening. He had just had time to grab a quick shower and a sandwich before leaving for this first training meeting. His adrenaline was still revved when he stepped into the cavernous garage-like space and studied the group arranged in an assortment of chairs and old furniture angled toward the front of the room.

He spotted a few faces familiar to him from the previous Saturday's rescue, but found himself searching for Chris. He spotted her in a far corner, at one end of a sofa, her dog, Harley, at her feet. He took the empty seat beside her. "Hello," he said.

She eyed him coolly. "Hey."

Harley approached and Rand petted the dog. He wanted the animal to trust him, even if his mistress didn't. "How are you?" he asked.

"Fine."

She wasn't exactly unfriendly, just…guarded. Which only made him want to break through her reserve more. "I saw some of your paintings at a restaurant in town," he said. "I really like your work."

"They're all for sale."

"I might buy one. I've always enjoyed landscapes, and yours are beautiful—but they're also complex." He glanced at her arm and the artwork there. She wore a sleeveless blouse, revealing a tapestry of colorful flowers and birds from shoulder to wrist on the arm closest to him. Columbines, bluebells, foxglove, a bluebird, and a gold finch. The scene reminded him of one of her paintings. And yes, there, just above her elbow, half-hidden between a dragonfly and a sunflower, a woman peered out with large dark eyes, hiding and watchful. "Mysterious."

"Hmmm. Not that I don't like it when people say nice things about my work, but it's not going to convince me to go out with you."

"Can't blame a man for trying." He smiled.

She looked away.

"Let's get started, everybody." Danny spoke from the front of the room, and the chatter died down. "I'll start by introducing our newest team member. Some of you already know Dr. Rand Martin, who assisted with our rescue of the injured hiker on Saturday. In addition to serving as our medical adviser, Rand has decided to join as a full-fledged volunteer."

Scattered applause from the gathered volunteers. Rand nodded. Danny continued, "Just so you know, Rand's a rookie, but he has a lot of experience. He served with a mobile surgical unit in Afghanistan and is the new director of emergency services at St. Joseph's Hospital in Junction."

More applause, and a few shouts of "Welcome!"

"You can introduce yourselves at the break," Danny said. "Now, let's get down to business." He consulted the clipboard in his hand and read off a list of upcoming training opportunities, certification deadlines and local news. "The sheriff asked me to remind everyone that the annual Back-country Base Camp rally is August 1 through 4. There's also a scout group from Denver planning a wilderness-skills camp up on Dakota Ridge starting August 5. Both of those groups could mean more calls for us."

"A bunch of kids playing with fire and knives?" a big man near the back of the room said. "What could go wrong?"

Danny smiled and waited for the chuckles to die down. "I'm going to turn it over to Tony now for our training unit on wilderness searches. For some of you this will be a review, but pay attention, because we have some new protocols based on the latest research. And for you newbies, know that you could be called to put this into practice any day now. We have a lot of wilderness we're responsible for, and it's easy for people to get lost out there."

Rand pulled out a notebook and pen and settled in as a tall, thin man, his blond hair and goatee threaded with silver, moved to the front of the room. Chris passed Rand a sheaf of handouts. "Pretty much everything is on these," she said.

"Thanks."

He pretended to study the first sheet of the handout, but he was really focused on her. She was more relaxed than she had been Saturday, but she still had the hyperawareness he recognized from his time in Afghanistan. In a war zone, chaos could break out at any second, even in the middle of dinner or when you were trying to sleep after a hard battle. Soldiers lived on high alert, and being in constant fight-or-flight mode took its toll physically and psychologically.

But Chris wasn't in a war zone. So why so tense?

The room darkened and Tony began his presentation.

Rand forced himself to concentrate on the lesson. Apparently, people who became lost tended to behave in established patterns depending on their age, gender and history. "Knowing these patterns doesn't guarantee we'll locate them," Tony said. "But it helps us establish a search plan and can increase the odds of finding them."

Rand underlined phrases on the handout and wrote notes in the margin. And here he had thought his training would consist of learning to tie knots and reviewing how to administer first aid. He was so absorbed in the material he had to shake himself out of a kind of trance when the lights went up again. He checked his watch and was surprised to find over an hour had passed.

"We'll break for ten minutes, then finish up this unit," Tony said.

Chairs slid back and the hum of conversation rose. Rand turned to address Chris, but she was already out of her chair and moving across the room. Danny waylaid her, and the two fell into earnest conversation. Curious, Rand worked his way toward them but was stopped by other volunteers who wanted to introduce themselves. He made small talk, all the while working his way over to Chris and Danny, who stood in the hallway outside the restrooms.

Rand positioned himself in front of a bulletin board around the corner from them and listened. "I'm sorry," Chris said. "I know I shouldn't have disappeared like that, but it was an emergency. I got a call from my mom. She's okay now, but I thought at first I was going to have to rush to her."

"I'm sorry to hear that," Danny said. "I've been in that position myself. But next time, let someone know. Send a text or something."

"I will. I promise."

"Are you sure that's all that's going on?" Danny asked.

"Of course." Rand thought he recognized a forced cheerfulness in her voice. He moved over to get a better look, and Chris collided with him as she came around the corner.

"Sorry," he said, steadying her with one hand but immediately releasing her. She was skittish as a wild colt, and he didn't want to upset her.

She stared up at him, eyes wide, then moved away. Rand watched her cross the room, half believing she would leave altogether. Instead, she stopped by a table of refreshments and began filling a plate.

She didn't return to her seat until Tony had resumed the lesson. She slid onto the sofa beside him just as the lights went down, as if she had timed her arrival to avoid further conversation.

When the evening ended, Rand started after her but was halted by a trio of men, including the big guy who had made the remark about the scouts. They introduced themselves as Eldon Ramsey, Ryan Welch and Caleb Garrison. "Have you done any climbing?" the big guy, Eldon, asked.

"Only a little," Rand asked.

"It's a skill that comes in handy on a lot of the rescues we're called out on," Ryan said. "You'll have training opportunities, but any time you want to get in some practice on your own, give us a shout."

"We're climbing in Caspar Canyon most weekends during the season," Caleb said. "Come on out and join us anytime."

"Thanks," Rand said. "I'll do that."

The instructor for the evening, Tony Meisner, introduced himself next, along with Sheri Stevens, Jake and Hannah

Gwynn, Grace Wilcox, and several others whose names Rand couldn't remember. Everyone was friendly and offered to help him in any way they could. By the time the building emptied out, Rand had accepted that he wasn't going to talk to Chris tonight. She would have left long ago.

Except, apparently, she hadn't. He spotted her and Harley walking across the parking lot and headed after her while trying to appear as if he wasn't in a hurry. She glanced over her shoulder at his approach but said nothing. The stiffness in her shoulders told him she was a few breaths from telling him to get lost. No sense wasting the opportunity with small talk. "Have you seen any more of the man who was watching you Saturday?" he asked.

She slowed her steps. "No. I must have been mistaken. He was looking at something else."

She didn't believe that, he thought.

"Mind if I walk you to your car?" he asked.

She shrugged. "Suit yourself."

Seconds later, they arrived at a dusty blue Subaru. She stopped and turned to him. Before she could say anything, he took a step back. "I'm not trying to be a creep or harass you," he said. "If you don't want to go out with me, that's your call. But I saw that guy on the trail Saturday and how you reacted to his attention. If you need help or you just want to talk to someone, I'm here. That's all I want you to know."

Some of the stiffness went out of her posture, and she looked at him with less suspicion. "Thanks," she said. "But it's not really anything you need to worry about." She clicked her key fob. The car beeped and flashed its lights, and she opened the rear driver's-side door. "In you go, Harley."

The dog started to jump into the car, then stopped and backed out, something in his mouth. "What has he got?" Rand leaned in for a closer look.

Chris took the object from the dog, and all the color left her face. She collapsed against the side of the car, eyes wide.

Rand took the item from her. It was a bird—a hummingbird, made of folded emerald green paper. "Is this origami?" he asked.

She nodded, the look on her face frantic now.

Still holding the paper bird, he reached for her. "Chris," he said.

But she turned away, clutching her stomach, and vomited on the gravel beside the car.

He pulled her close, half-afraid she would collapse. She leaned heavily against him, shudders running through her. "Tell me why you're so upset," he said.

"I can't."

Seventeen Years Ago

TEN-YEAR-OLD CHRIS was seated at a folding table in a cold, drafty room, a stack of colored paper in front of her—pink, blue, red, orange, purple, green. Pretty colors, but looking at them didn't make Chris happy. No one called her Chris then. They knew her as Elita. She willed away tears as she painstakingly folded and smoothed the paper to make a hummingbird like the model in front of her. "You need five thousand of them," the woman across from her—Helen—said. "You will make some every day. And when you are done, it will be time."

Tears slipped past her tight-closed lids and made a hot

path down her cheeks. She tried to wipe them away, hoping Helen hadn't seen. "What if I can't make five thousand of them?" she asked. It seemed an impossibly large number.

"You will. You have a couple of years. It will take that long until you're ready for the duties ahead of you."

Chris shuddered. She didn't want to think about those "duties." Not that she had a terribly clear idea what those might include, but she had heard whispers...

She made a wrong fold, and the paper creased, the hummingbird crumpling in her hand. Helen took the mangled paper from her. "Start with a fresh sheet. Pay attention, and take your time."

"Maybe I can't do it because I'm not the right person," Chris said. "Maybe I'm not worthy."

Helen smiled. "You are the right person. You have been chosen."

Choose someone else! Chris wanted to shout. But she only bit her lip as another tear betrayed her.

Helen frowned. "You should be happy you have been singled out for such an honor. You shouldn't be so ungrateful."

"I'm... I'm not," she lied, and bit the inside of her cheek. Anything to stem the tears. She couldn't let Helen see what her true feelings were. Even at her young age, she knew that was dangerous.

"Chris." Rand snapped his fingers in front of her face. "What's going on? Why are you so afraid?"

"I have to go." She pushed him aside and slid into the car. Harley bolted in after her, climbing over Chris and settling in the passenger seat. Rand was talking to her, but she couldn't hear him over the buzzing panic in her head. She drove away, gripping the steering wheel so tightly her fingers ached. She checked her mirrors every few seconds, but no one appeared to be following her.

When she was in her parking space in the alley behind the gallery, she made sure the doors of her car were locked, then laid her head on the steering wheel and closed her eyes, her whole body trembling. She never had made the five thousand hummingbirds. She had believed getting away had ended her ordeal.

But someone had pushed that bird through the gap in her car window. When she had parked at search and rescue headquarters, she thought the lot was safe enough for her to leave the rear windows down just a few inches to keep the interior cool. Jedediah, or someone else, had taken advantage of that, letting her know she could never truly escape. They were telling her it was time to fulfill what they thought was her destiny. The one thing she was determined never to do.

Chapter Four

Early Saturday morning, Rand drove home from Junction. He had been called in after midnight to tend to a young man who had suffered multiple injuries as a result of wrapping his car around a tree along a curvy road—fractured sternum, broken ribs and collarbone, a fractured arm, and multiple bruises and cuts. Rand had spent hours wiring the man's bones back together. Weariness set in when he was halfway home, so he did what he always did to try to stay awake: he opened a window to let in fresh air and thought about something other than himself and his fatigue.

He had stayed away from Chris since Thursday night, even though the desire to know what was going on with her gnawed at him, a low-level ache. If she wanted his help, she would ask. To keep pressing himself on her could be seen as harassment. He wanted to be her friend, not someone else she was afraid of.

He thought of the origami hummingbird. Not exactly a threatening item, yet Chris had been physically ill at the sight of it. He had a bad feeling about that moment, but maybe he was putting too much of himself and his own history into it. Maybe the hummingbird had been a kind of sick joke that only had meaning to her, not a real threat.

But could anyone be so upset by a joke that they would throw up?

His phone vibrated, and seconds later the video screen on his dash showed he had an incoming text. He pressed the button to hear the message, and the car's mechanical female voice recited, "Wildfire on national forest land south end of County Road 3. All search and rescue volunteers needed to evacuate campers in the area."

Rand increased his speed and headed toward search and rescue headquarters. He parked and joined the crowd of volunteers just inside. He spotted Chris right away, her blue hair standing out in the sea of blondes and brunettes. "Hello," she said when he approached. No animosity. No particular warmth either.

"What should I do to help?" he asked.

She shoved a lidded plastic bin into his hands. "Put these first aid supplies in the Beast." She indicated a boxy orange Jeep with oversize tires and a red cross on the back door. "And do whatever Danny or whoever he appoints as incident commander tells you."

He joined a line of volunteers passing gear to the vehicles, then followed Ryan and Caleb to a Toyota truck. He, Caleb and Carrie Andrews squeezed into the back seat. Ryan drove, and Eldon took the passenger seat. They followed the Beast to the highway, then turned onto a county road that grew progressively narrower and bumpier as they climbed in elevation.

"Check out the smoke," Eldon said, and pointed at the windshield to a black plume rising in the distance.

"People who don't live here don't understand how dangerous these dry conditions are," Ryan said. "One spark from a campfire or a discarded cigarette can set a blaze that destroys hundreds of thousands of acres."

Ahead of them, the orange Jeep slowed, then pulled over to the side and stopped. Ryan pulled his truck in behind it and rolled down the window. The headlights of a vehicle moved toward them. Tony stepped out from the driver's side of the Jeep and flagged down the vehicle. Rand leaned his head out the open back window to hear the conversation. A second car idled behind the first. The driver of the first—a man perhaps in his fifties, his brown hair heavily streaked with white—spoke clearly enough for Rand to hear.

"Are you with the campers who are back here?" Danny asked.

"I don't know about that," the man said.

"Were you camped in the national forest?" Danny tried again.

"Yes. We saw the smoke getting heavier and decided to leave."

"How many are with you?" Danny glanced toward the other vehicle.

"There are six of us here."

"Only six?" Danny asked.

"More'll be along soon," the man said. "They're packing up camp."

"How many people?" Danny's tone signaled that he was quickly losing patience with the man's casual attitude.

"Maybe a dozen."

"Men? Women? Children?"

"What business is that of yours?" the driver asked.

"Whoever is back there needs to get out now," Danny said. "They don't have time to pack. The winds are pushing the fire this way. We're here to help with the evacuation."

"They're just a few miles back," the man said. "You won't have any trouble finding them." He shifted the car into gear and lurched forward, the other vehicle close on his bumper. As they passed, Rand got a glimpse through tinted glass of two adults in the first vehicle and four in the second. All men, he thought.

Tony climbed back into the Beast, and the caravan of volunteers set out again, driving a little faster now, their sense of urgency heightened by the thickening smoke. "Do we know anything about these campers?" Rand asked after a moment. "Who they are or where they're from?"

"Danny said he got a call from the sheriff that one of the spotters in a plane flying over the fire saw a group of tents in a clearing and called it in," Caleb said. "Cell phone coverage is spotty to nonexistent back in here, so they might not have realized the fire had even started."

"No missing all this smoke," Eldon said. "Anyone with any sense would know to get out of Dodge by now."

The Jeep stopped again, this time in the middle of the road. Ryan halted the truck, too, and everyone piled out. Smoke stung Rand's eyes, and the scent of burning wood hung heavy in the air. "There's active flames ahead," Tony said. "We can't go any further or we risk getting trapped. We need to turn around."

"What about the other campers?" Carrie asked. "The driver of the car said there were others."

Danny glanced over his shoulder. Smoke obscured the road ahead, though occasional orange flares illuminated burning trees. "We don't know who or how many are in there," he said. "We can't put our own lives at risk. That doesn't help anyone."

Rand wanted to volunteer to go ahead on foot to scout

the situation. But then what? He could end up injured or trapped, and the other volunteers might feel obligated to go in after him. But he hated this feeling of helplessness and defeat.

"Hello? Help! Oh, please help!"

They turned toward the sound as a woman stumbled down the road toward them. She was almost bent double beneath what Rand thought at first was a large pack but turned out to be a child wrapped in a sleeping bag, clinging to her back. As they rushed toward her, other figures emerged from the smoke—more women, half a dozen children and a single man, all carrying supplies and bundles of clothing, bedding, and who knew what else.

The lone man brought up the rear of the group. He had a blanket roll on his back and a large wooden box in his arms. "The truck broke down, and we had to walk," he said, his words cut short by a fit of coughing.

Rand stared at the collection of women and children— some with soot on their faces, holes from sparks burned in their clothing—and thought of the men in the two cars. They had left women and children to *walk* out of a fire?

He flinched at a crack like a gunshot, then realized it was a tree not thirty yards away, bursting into flame. "We have to get out of here," Danny said. He took the nearest woman's arm. "Into the vehicles. Drop whatever you're carrying and get in. You'll have to sit on laps, on the floorboards—wherever you can fit."

Another woman spoke up. "That isn't necessary." She seemed a little taller than the others, but maybe it was only that she stood straighter and looked them in the eye when she spoke. "We will carry our possessions and walk out."

"You can't walk fast enough to stay ahead of the fire," Danny said.

"We have divine protection."

The words snapped Rand's patience. "Get in the trucks now!" he shouted. He picked up the closest child and shoved them into the back seat of the truck.

Caleb and Ryan reached for other children. Eldon picked up a woman and deposited her in the front passenger seat. Others began relieving the stranded campers of their burdens and leading them to the vehicles. They seemed to come out of their trance then. The man and several of the women and older children crowded into the back of the truck.

"What about our things?" one of the women wailed.

"We don't have room for them," Tony said.

She began to cry. Others were already weeping, children screaming.

"Is there anyone else?" Danny asked. He had to raise his voice above the din . "Any stragglers we should wait for?"

"No." The man shook his head. "No one."

Rand hoped the man was telling the truth. The flames were near enough he could feel the heat now, smoke so heavy he could no longer make out the road, the roar of the fire so loud they had to shout to be heard. A hot wind swirled around them, sparks stinging bare skin and smoldering on clothing. They didn't have time to search for anyone who might have been left behind.

Somehow, they managed to turn the vehicles and head back down the road, forced by poor visibility to creep along yet driving as fast as they dared in order to escape the flames. Everyone was coughing now, everyone's eyes streaming tears.

They slowed to steer around a burning tree that had

fallen on the side of the road, and the weight in the back of the truck shifted. The wailing rose in pitch, and Rand looked back to see that the man had jumped from the truck and was running down the road, back in the direction they had come. He had his hand on the door, about to open it, when Caleb gripped his arm. "Let him go. We have to save the rest."

Rand forced his body to relax and nodded. Even if he had wanted, he couldn't have exited the vehicle. He was held down by a child on each thigh, a boy and a girl, who were about nine or ten. They sat stiffly and wouldn't meet his gaze, hands clenched in front of them, eyes downcast. Obviously, they were terrified. Traumatized. Maybe that explained why they weren't acting like any children he had ever met.

After what felt like the longest ride of his life but was probably only half an hour, they arrived at the staging area on the picnic grounds at the turnoff for the county road. Paramedics, the sheriff and his deputies, and other volunteers surrounded the Beast and the truck, someone taking charge of each of the campers as they emerged. "We found them trying to walk out of the fire," Danny explained to the sheriff.

Sheriff Travis Walker was a tall man in his midthirties, with dark hair and eyes, a sharply pressed khaki uniform, and a grim expression on his face. "Any idea what a bunch of women and children were doing camping back in there with no transportation?" he asked.

"There was a man with them," Ryan said. "He bailed out of the truck and ran back in the direction of the camp not long after we set out."

"There were six other men, in two vehicles," Tony said.

"We passed them on the way out. They told us they had left the others—" he nodded at the women and children "—to pack up the camp and follow."

The sheriff's frown deepened. "We'll question them later, find out what's going on."

"I think they might belong to some kind of cult," Rand said.

Everyone turned to stare at him. "What makes you say that?" Travis asked.

"One of the women told us they weren't worried about the fire because they were under 'divine protection.' That, and the fact that a group of able-bodied men, probably the leaders, left a bunch of women and children to fend for themselves, and the women aren't questioning—at least not out loud—their right to do so. Blind obedience that goes against all common sense is one hallmark of a cult."

Thankfully, the sheriff didn't ask how Rand knew this. "We'll question them and find out as much as we can," he said.

"How do you know that? About cults?"

Rand tensed at the familiar voice and turned to look at Chris.

"My sister was in a cult," he said. "I learned a lot about them when we were trying to persuade her to leave."

"Did she leave?" Chris stared at him, lips parted, leaning toward him as if something important depended on his answer.

He shook his head. "No. She never did."

Her expression softened, and she put her hand on his arm. A familiar tightness rose in his throat, but he forced himself not to turn away. He didn't see pity in Chris's eyes, but some other emotion, one he couldn't quite read.

And then she whirled away from him, propelled by a hand on her shoulder. The driver of the car they had met in the burning forest stood with two other men, all crowded around Chris.

Rand moved in behind her, but the men ignored him. All three were middle-aged, from the fortysomething blond Rand had seen on the trail a week ago to the slightly older driver of the car, to a shorter, red-faced man with a round, boyish face but iron gray hair who stood between them. "Hello, Elita," the driver said.

"My name isn't Elita," Chris said. But her voice trembled.

"Your time has come," the blond said.

"I don't know what you're talking about." She tried to turn away, but the blond grabbed her.

Rand took the man's wrist and squeezed, hard, his thumb digging in between the fine bones in a way that was guaranteed to hurt. The man released her but turned on Rand. "This is no business of yours," he said.

"Don't touch her again," Rand said. He kept his voice low, but anyone would know he meant business. He was dimly aware that a crowd had gathered, among them the sheriff and one of his deputies.

The blond turned back to Chris. "You can't deny your destiny," he said. He glanced at those around them and raised his voice so that it carried to everyone. "We will start the wedding preparations today."

Chapter Five

Sheriff Walker stepped forward. "What is your name?" he asked the driver.

The blond spoke first. "This doesn't concern you, Sheriff," he said.

Travis's expression didn't change. "The three of you need to come to the sheriff's department and provide statements about the fire and how it started."

"We don't know how it started," the round-faced man said. "That has nothing to do with us."

"I also want to know why the three of you left a group of women and children to make their way out of the area on foot," Travis said.

The blond man moved closer. He was taller than the others, not large, but imposing. "We left a man in charge of the women and children," he said. "Joshua was bringing them in the truck." He looked around. "Where is Joshua?"

"The man who was with the women and children ran back into the woods," Rand said.

The blond shifted his attention to Rand. "Who are you?" It wasn't a question as much as a demand.

"I'm one of the volunteers who helped save those women and children you abandoned," Rand said.

The man glared at him but addressed the sheriff. "You

need to talk to Joshua. I can't help you." He turned away, and the others started to follow him.

"Before you leave, I need your names and contact information," the sheriff said.

The blond man nodded to the round-faced man. He pulled a small case from his pocket and handed the sheriff a business card. "That's the name of our attorney," he said. "You can contact him."

The three walked away. Travis pocketed the card and glanced over as his brother, Sergeant Gage Walker, joined the group. "The car is registered to something called the Vine, LLC," he said.

Travis turned to Chris. She had remained silent since the men had approached, pale and still. "What do you know about this?" he asked.

She swallowed hard. "The blond man is named Jedediah," she said. "I don't know his last name. He works for a man named Edmund Harrison, though most people know him as the Exalted. He leads the Vine. I don't know the other two, but they're probably part of the Exalted's inner circle— the ones charged with keeping order within the group."

"What is the Vine?" Gage asked. "Some kind of vineyard or something?"

Chris shook her head. "The Vine is, well, I guess you'd say it's a cult. A kind of religion, but not exactly. Edmund Harrison is the leader, the Exalted."

"What's your connection to the group?" Travis asked.

She stared at the ground. "My mother and father were members—a long time ago. My father died, and after that…" She paused. Rand could sense her struggling to control her emotions. Her shoulders drew inward, and she clenched her hands tightly. But after a long moment, she lifted her head. "My mother broke with the group when I was twelve. I haven't seen or heard from them since."

She was lying. Rand was sure of it. She had seen Jedediah on the trail last Saturday and had recognized him. And he had recognized her.

"What was all that about a wedding?" Ryan asked. "And why did he call you by that other name—Lisa or something?"

"Elita." She blew out a breath. "It's a long story."

"I'd like you to come to my office and tell me about it," Travis said. "If it turns out they were responsible for that fire, or the death of anyone in it, I need to know as much about them as possible."

"I'll come with you," Rand said.

Chris turned to him, and he braced himself for her to tell him to back off, that this was none of his business. "You don't have to do this alone," he said softly. Whatever was behind this, the encounter had clearly shaken her. He wanted to be there to lend her strength. To take away a little of her fear.

She nodded. "All right."

"We can go now," Travis said. "I want to get your statement before Jedediah and the others have a chance to get too far away."

"They won't go far," Chris said. "Not until they have me. I'm the reason they're here."

Eighteen years ago

"WE'VE COME TODAY to reveal that Elita has been selected for an amazing honor."

Elita had been trying to teach herself to knit by following the illustrations in a library book when the two women and one man had knocked on the door of the travel trailer where she and her mother and father lived, on the edge of an apple grove owned by the Vine. The trailer was old—hot in the summer and cold in the winter, and when it rained, the roof over Elita's bunk bed leaked—but they had lived here since Elita was five years old, and she was nine now.

She hadn't been called *Elita* when they'd first moved here. She had been Christine Elizabeth back then. But one day, not long after they had arrived, her father had announced they were all taking new names. Her new name was Elita. "It means 'the chosen one,'" he told her. "The Exalted himself named you. It's a very special honor."

She thought it was strange to suddenly have a new name, but she knew better than to argue, and over time, she got used to being Elita instead of Christine.

The woman who spoke, Helen, was older than Elita's mom. She had long brown hair almost to her waist, the strands glinting with silver, and pale blue eyes. She oversaw the Sunday school Elita attended, and whenever she smiled at Elita, the little girl felt warm and happy.

The other woman, Sarai, was older and sour-faced. She taught the younger children and carried a switch when she walked between the rows of students, and didn't hesitate to pop them on the back of the hand if they gave a wrong answer to her questions. Elita didn't like her, and she avoided looking at her now.

But the man—Jedediah—was the one who really frightened her. The way he watched everyone, especially the girls, made her feel sick to her stomach. He was supposed to be one of the holiest among them, serving as the Exalted's right hand. But to her, he seemed evil.

Elita's mother—whom everyone called Lana now, though she had been born Amy—came and stood behind Elita, resting both hands on her shoulders. "This is a surprise," she said. "Why would Elita be singled out for an honor?"

"She has found favor with the Exalted," Helen said. She smiled at Elita, but this time the little girl didn't feel warm or happy. She felt cold and scared. Like Jedediah, the Exalted frightened her. Not because he was mean or creepy, but because everyone acted afraid of him, and there were a lot of rules about how to behave around him. Not just anyone could speak to the Exalted. And her mother had told her once that the best way to behave around the Exalted was to pretend to be invisible. Elita hadn't understood what she meant. People couldn't be invisible.

Mom's hands tightened on her shoulders. "What is this great honor?" she asked.

"The Exalted has chosen Elita to be his bride." Helen said the words with a breathless awe, her cheeks flushed and eyes alight.

Elita's mother gasped. "She's only nine years old."

"It isn't to happen right away," Helen said. "There will be years for her to prepare. But when she has reached maturity, there will be a grand wedding."

Her father moved in to stand beside them. He patted Elita's shoulder and smiled when she looked up at him. "This is indeed an honor," he said. "Thank the Exalted for us."

"But the Exalted is already married," Elita said. She had seen his wife, Miracle, seated beside him at the ceremonies. And they had children—four of them, all blond like Miracle.

"Yes." Helen turned to Elita, no longer smiling. "The Exalted has chosen you as his second wife."

Her mother's fingers were digging into Elita's shoulders now. "That is indeed a great honor," she said carefully. "But Elita is so young. Surely there are other, more suitable women…"

"He has chosen Elita," Jedediah said, his voice overly loud in the small space. Harsh. "How dare you question his choice."

"I meant no disrespect," Mom said, and bowed her head. But Elita could feel her trembling.

"Of course she doesn't," her father said. "And it's good that Elita has been chosen now. She will have years to learn all she will need to know for such an honored position."

"Of course," Helen said. She smiled at Elita once more. "We have much to do to prepare you for your future role."

"What does she need to do?" Mom asked.

"I will instruct her myself," Helen said. "I will teach her all she needs to know to be a fitting bride for our Exalted leader." She took a step back. "I'm sure you are both in awe. I will leave you to ponder your good fortune."

She and Sarai turned and left, but Jedediah stayed behind. He fixed them with a hard gaze: "Don't think you're going to get out of this," he said. "Remember what happened to Elim."

As soon as the door closed behind him, Elita's mother sank to her knees. Elita sat beside her. "Mom, what's wrong?" she asked.

Her mother pulled her close and stroked her hair. "I won't let anyone hurt you," she whispered.

"They're not going to hurt her," her father said. "This is a great honor."

"She's a child," her mother said, her expression fierce. "And if she does decide to marry one day, she should be free to make her own choice. The idea of her being married off to some old man who already has one wife—it's positively medieval."

"The Old Testament kings all had many wives," her father said.

"The Exalted is not an Old Testament king. And I can't believe you're going along with this."

Her father's expression sagged, and he looked away. "I don't see that we have any choice," he said. "No one goes against the Exalted's decrees."

"When we came here, it was because the Vine offered a better way of life—one full of cooperation and peace and contributing positive things to the world. No one ever said anything about marrying off children."

"She's not going to marry him right away," her father said. "The wedding will be years away, and anything could happen before then."

"We could leave," her mother said.

"We can't leave." He leaned closer and lowered his voice, as if Elita wasn't sitting right there between them. "You heard what Jedediah said—about Elim."

"Who's Elim?" Elita asked.

"Just…someone who used to belong to the Vine," her mother said.

"What happened to him?" Elita asked.

"He went away," her father said. "But we aren't going anywhere." He sounded almost angry. Elita leaned against her mom, trying to make herself smaller.

"We're going to take care of Elita," her mother said. "We're going to do whatever it takes to look after her." Her mother sounded angry, too, and Elita felt like crying. Whatever was going on was Jedediah's fault. And maybe the Exalted's fault too. Though she would never say that out loud. Everyone—even kids like her—knew that you didn't say anything bad about the Exalted. She didn't know what would happen to her if she did, but she was pretty sure it would be terrible.

"MY PARENTS JOINED the Vine when I was five." Chris was calmer now, seated next to Rand in an interview room at the sheriff's department, several hours after the confrontation in the woods. Travis and Gage Walker sat across from them—looking as relaxed as two uniformed lawmen could, she thought. She ran a hand through her bright blue hair. "They met some members at the ice-cream shop they owned in town and liked what they had to say and ended up selling everything and moving into a mobile home on some land the Vine owned. Or maybe the group was squatting on the land. I don't really know. Anyway, things were fine until the year I turned nine."

When she didn't continue, Travis prodded her. "What happened when you were nine?"

"One of the women who was close to the Exalted, came to my parents and told them that the Exalted had decided that I would be his second wife."

"When you were *nine*?" Rand didn't try to hide his shock.

She nodded. "The wedding wasn't going to take place until I was older. My dad told me it wouldn't happen until I was all grown up, and by then I would be looking forward to it. He went along with the idea that I'd been chosen for a great honor, but my mom didn't feel that way. I remember they argued about it."

The old sadness returned as she remembered the tense

atmosphere in her family in the days after the announcement. "I had to take classes from a woman named Helen. Things like etiquette, and I had to memorize a lot of the Exalted's sayings. They were like proverbs, I guess. And I had to learn to sew and cook and read poetry. I was just a kid, and I thought a lot of it was dumb and boring, yet it didn't really feel dangerous or anything. But my mom really didn't like me taking the classes. My dad thought they wouldn't hurt anything, so they fought about that too." She sighed. "Things went along like that until I turned twelve. Then Jedediah and Helen showed up one evening and announced that the wedding would take place in a couple of weeks."

"When you were twelve," Rand clarified.

"Yes." She swallowed, recalling the details of that day. Details these people didn't need to hear. No one spoke, waiting. She could feel their eyes on her, especially Rand's. It was as if everyone in the room was holding their breath in anticipation of her next words. "My father died the day after that announcement was made. My mother said he tried to convince the Exalted that I was too young. The official story was that Dad died from eating poisonous mushrooms, but my mom and I always believed he was killed for getting in the way of something the Exalted wanted."

She studied her hands on the table, fingers laced together, reliving those awful days.

"You think someone in the group murdered your father?" Travis asked.

"Yes. But we don't have any proof, and my mom was too afraid to say anything. A few days later, she and I ran away."

"No one came after you?" Gage asked.

"They came looking for us," Chris said. "We knew they would. For years, we kept bags packed, and we would move every time we saw anyone we recognized from the Vine. Then, for a long time, we didn't see anyone. I thought we had gotten away." She glanced at Rand. "Until I saw Jedediah on the trail that day. I knew he recognized me, and it would be only a matter of time."

"He can't force you to marry someone," Travis said.

"The law may say he can't, but the Vine makes their own laws," she said.

"Have you found out anything more about these people?" Rand asked the sheriff. "Do they have any kind of criminal record?"

"We contacted the lawyer on the business card we were given," Travis said. "He declined to identify any of the principals in the Vine, LLC. We'll run a check on Edmund Harrison."

"Can you charge them in connection with the fire?" Rand asked.

"The fire appears to have started from a lightning strike. We haven't located the man you and others saw running away, back toward camp. No one else was harmed. Right now they haven't broken any laws."

"No one within the group will give evidence against them," Chris said. "They're either true believers who can't imagine the Exalted would ever do anything wrong or they're too afraid to speak out. And Harrison and those closest to him are careful."

"Have they made any specific threats to you?" Travis asked.

She shook her head. "Nothing more than what you heard, and that was more of a statement than a threat."

"That they would begin the wedding preparations today," Rand said. "But they can't force you to marry someone against your will."

"They believe they can." She hugged her arms across the chest. "They might try to kidnap me or drug me or threaten me. I don't know. I don't want to find out."

"If they do threaten you or try to force you to come with them, contact me." Travis handed her a business card. "Until then, there's not a lot we can do."

"I understand." She shoved back her chair. "If that's all, I'd like to go home now."

WHEN SHE STOOD, Rand rose also and followed her out. On the sidewalk, she turned to face him. "Thanks for the moral support, but I'm fine," she said. "I've dealt with these people most of my life. I know how to take care of myself."

"What are you going to do?" he asked.

"That's none of your business." She turned and started walking away.

She was right, but he followed her anyway. "Don't let them frighten you away."

"You don't know anything about it," she said, and kept walking.

"I know that you were strong enough to get away from them once," he said. "They may not like it, but it gives you the upper hand. You could expose them for what they really are and maybe save others."

"I just want them to leave me alone."

"I want that too. But I want more. I want to stop them from ruining other lives."

She halted alongside her Subaru, keys in hand. He

stopped, too, five feet away, giving her space but hoping she would listen. "Why do you even care?" she asked.

"Because I like you. And I don't want you to leave when we've just met."

She shook her head and opened the driver's-side door of the car. "Sorry to disappoint you," she said.

"And because I didn't do enough to help my sister."

She stilled, holding her position for a long, breathless moment, until at last she lifted her head and met his gaze. "You mean, you couldn't persuade her to leave," she said. "But that was her decision to make, if she was an adult."

"I should have dragged her away from them when I had the chance," he said. "I'll never get over that regret, but I can help others now."

"You can't make someone leave that lifestyle unless they want to," she said.

"I should have at least tried." His face was flushed, his breathing ragged. "We tried for two years to persuade her to leave, but she wouldn't. And then we found out she had committed suicide." He could say the words now without the stabbing pain they had once caused, but the hurt would never completely go away.

"I'm sorry," she said, her previous anger replaced by softness.

"So am I. And I'm sorry there was nothing we could do to stop that cult from ensnaring others. But I'll do anything I can to help you stop the Vine."

"What do you think we could do?"

"I don't know. But if they're really going to stay around here until you go with them, that gives us a little time to find out what else they've been up to. And if they do come after you, we'll stop them."

"I'm not sure they can be stopped," she said. "They have a lot of money, and that gives them power."

"Does that give them power over you?"

She didn't hesitate in her reply. "No."

"And they don't have any power over me." He moved closer until he was standing right in front of her. "Together, maybe we can find a way to stop them from hurting anyone else."

"All right." She slid into the car. "I need time to think. And to talk to my mom. She might know or remember something that can help us."

"Call me," he said.

She nodded and started the engine.

He stepped back and watched her leave, his stomach in knots. It was easy to make bold declarations about stopping these people, but all the talk in the world hadn't saved his sister.

Chapter Six

Chris gripped her phone tightly and paced her small living room as she told her mother about that morning's encounter with the Exalted's followers. "They walked right up and said all that about planning a wedding—in front of my friends and the sheriff and everyone. Now I know they all think I'm a freak."

Harley sat up on his bed by the sofa and watched her, forehead wrinkled in what seemed to Chris to be an expression of worry.

"It doesn't matter what they think of you," April said. "You can't let the Vine get you in their clutches again."

"I know that, Mom. And I'm being careful."

"Now that they've found you, they won't give up until they have you back," April said. "You need to leave."

Leaving had been Chris's first thought too. But Rand's plea wasn't the only thing that had stopped her from packing up and fleeing. "I have a good life here," she said. "I'm tired of running."

"Then come stay with me for a while. Just until they give up and leave town."

"And risk leading them to you? No." Her mother had worked hard to get away from the Vine. She had changed her name, her job, and her appearance, and kept a low profile in a small town in Ohio. Chris stopped at the window that looked down into the alley below. Her car was parked there, next to a large trash bin. Otherwise, the alley was empty. "I talked to the local sheriff today," she said. "I told him about Dad."

"He'll never find evidence that he was murdered," her mother said. "The Vine would make sure of that."

"I know we buried Dad in the woods," Chris said. "But I don't remember much about it."

"There was a funeral. The Exalted gave the eulogy, which was supposed to be a great honor. I don't remember anything he said."

"That didn't strike you as odd—that no law enforcement was called, or a local coroner, or anything?"

"No. We didn't involve outsiders. Our motto was that we took care of our own. Now I can see how that allowed the group to get away with horrible things, but at the time it seemed perfectly normal."

"There's a doctor here. He works with search and rescue, and he was there when Jedediah and two other men confronted me. Rand—the doctor—said if I stay, he'll help me fight the Vine."

"He doesn't know anything about them. He's probably just trying to impress you."

"He said his sister belonged to a cult. She committed suicide. He wants to keep them from hurting anyone else." She could still feel the impact of Rand's confession. He hadn't dismissed the idea that strangers would try to force her to marry or that she might be in danger from a harmless-looking back-to-nature group. He knew the power groups like the Vine could wield.

"Do you trust him?" April asked.

Chris didn't trust anyone. It had never felt safe to do so. "I believe he's sincere," she said. That wasn't the same as trust, exactly, but it was more than she could say about many of the people she'd met.

"Then let him help you. But don't depend on him."

"I know, Mom. The only person I can depend on is myself." How often had she repeated those words over the years? But they didn't make her feel stronger—only more alone.

"And me," April said. "You know I'll help you any way I can."

Harley stood and whined. Chris glanced at the dog. "I need to go now, Mom. I'll keep you posted on what happens here."

"I'll meet you anywhere, anytime you need me," April said. "I love you."

"I love you, too, Mom." She ended the call. Harley paced, the hair on the back of his neck and along his spine standing up. He let out a low growl and trotted over to the door.

Chris was on her way to the door when she heard footsteps in the hallway. Heart pounding, she checked the peephole. Jedediah's grim features glared back at her. Then he pounded on the door.

"Go away!" she said.

"We need to talk."

"I have nothing to say to you."

"The Exalted wants to see you."

"I don't have anything to say to him either. Go away."

"I'm here to take you to him."

"I'm calling the sheriff right now," she said, and pulled her phone from her pocket. She hit the nine and the one, then watched as Jedediah turned and left.

She sank to her knees and wrapped her arms around Harley, who still trembled with agitation. When she felt a little calmer, she focused on her phone once more. She didn't call 911. Instead, she selected the number she had programmed into the phone only that afternoon.

"Chris? Is everything okay?" Rand sounded a little out of breath. She tried to picture him, perhaps in doctor's scrubs. Or would he be at home?

"Jedediah was just here," she said.

"Did you call the sheriff?"

"I told him I would, so he left. I just… I wanted someone to know." Someone who might understand.

"I'm at the hospital in Junction. Is there someone else you can call to stay with you?"

"No, I'm okay. I have Harley. He let me know Jedediah was here before he even got to the door."

"What happened?" Rand asked. "What did he say to you?"

"He told me the Exalted wants to see me. I told him I didn't have anything to say to him, and then I said I was going to call the sheriff. He left. It's almost funny, really, that he thought I would meekly come with him. As if I was still nine years old."

"If he comes back, don't waste time talking to him," Rand said. "Dial 911 right away."

"I will. I won't keep you any longer. I'll see you at the training tonight."

"I'll pick you up, and we can go together," he said.

She started to protest, then imagined parking in that alley in the dark. It would be so easy for Jedediah and others to grab her. "All right," she said. "Thanks."

She ended the call and stood. Harley followed her to

the desk in the corner, where Chris opened her laptop. She would write down everything she knew about the Vine and do some research online to learn whatever she could. Some people said knowledge was power. She would need every advantage to defeat someone like the Exalted, who was so accustomed to getting his own way.

RAND CHANGED OUT of his scrubs and made a quick stop at his house before he drove to pick up Chris. He removed his Sig Sauer M17 from the safe, loaded it and slipped it into his pocket. He didn't trust the members of the Vine not to come after Chris again, and he wanted to be prepared.

He parked in the alley next to Chris's Subaru and waited a moment after he shut off the engine, searching the darkness outside the circle of light cast by the single bulb over the door leading to the stairs to Chris's apartment. Nothing moved within those shadows, so he pulled out his phone and texted Chris. On my way up.

She met him at the door, her dog by her side. Harley eyed him warily but made no sound as Rand said hello, then offered the back of his hand for a sniff. "Good dog," Chris praised, rubbing behind the ridgeback's ear. "I'm ready to go," she said, and picked up her keys.

He waited while she locked her door, then preceded her down the steps, pausing to check the alley before he stepped out in it. He was a little surprised at how easily he slipped back into this mode of being on patrol, as if he was back in Afghanistan, where something as simple as walking to the latrine could make you a target.

Chris said nothing as she stood close behind him, then hurried after him to his car, head down. Harley followed, and hopped into the back seat of Rand's SUV. "I couldn't leave him," she said of the dog. "I'm too afraid Jedediah or someone else might try to hurt him."

"No problem," Rand said. "I like dogs."

She remained silent all the way to search and rescue headquarters. The brightness of the room and the hum of conversation was jarring after the tension in his car, but he felt her relax as she sank into the end of the sofa and took out a notebook and pen. He sat beside her and did the same but couldn't shed his wariness as easily.

"Hey, Chris, how are you doing?"

"Everything okay, Chris?"

"Hey, Chris. You good?"

One by one, the gathered volunteers made a point to stop by and say hello. Those who hadn't been at the call-out for the fire would have heard about Chris's encounter with the members of the Vine. None of them asked any questions, though Rand read the curiosity in their eyes.

Chris accepted the attention calmly. "I'm good, thanks," she told anyone who inquired.

An elfin young woman with a cloud of dark curls approached. "Hey, Chris, how are you doing?" she asked. "I've been meaning to tell you how much I love your hair. And your tattoos." She glanced at her own bare arms. "I've been thinking of getting a tattoo myself, but my mom would probably have a heart attack if I did, and my three brothers would lose their minds." She grinned, deep dimples forming on either side of her mouth. "Which is kind of why I want to do it."

"Bethany, this is Rand," Chris said.

"Hey, Rand." Bethany offered her hand. "I'm glad you joined the group. For one thing, it means I'm no longer the newest rookie." She bent and patted Harley. "I miss my dog," she said. "But when I moved here my parents wouldn't let me take Charlie with me. I think they thought if they said that, I wouldn't leave, but they were wrong about that."

"Where are you from?" Rand asked, as much to spare Chris from the steady stream of chatter as out of genuine curiosity.

"Waterbury, Vermont. I'm one of four and the only girl. To say that my parents and brothers are overprotective is an understatement. I practically had an armed guard with me everywhere I went. Living here, by myself, is a whole new experience."

Sheri Stevens took her place at the front of the room. "I better get to my seat," Bethany said. "I just wanted to say hi. Maybe we can get together for coffee or a drink sometime."

Before Chris could answer, she was gone.

"She's certainly friendly," Rand said.

"She's a little overwhelming," Chris said.

"All right, everyone. Let's focus on this evening's topic of wilderness first aid," Sheri began. "This will be a review for some of you, but it's a requirement, and standard practices do get updated from time to time, so pay attention."

Rand figured he could have taught the class, given his experiences in a field hospital, though he hoped a local search and rescue group would never have to deal with treating people who had been hit by improvised explosives or sniper fire. His mind drifted to his fellow volunteers. He didn't know most of them very well, but he was impressed that they would give so much time and attention to helping others, most of whom were probably strangers passing through the area, on vacation or on their way to somewhere else.

After an hour, they took a break. Ryan and Caleb joined

him and Chris at the refreshment table. "We think that group that escaped the fire is camping out at Davis Draw," Ryan said. He picked up a peanut butter cookie and bit into it.

"Where is Davis Draw?" Chris asked. She didn't look alarmed.

"It's off a forest service road at the end of County Road 14," Caleb said. "It's not as nice as the area where they were—less trees, mostly desert scrub. And they'll have to haul water."

"How did you find this out?" Chris asked. She stirred sugar into a cup of coffee.

"We drove out there and saw a bunch of trailers and big tents," Ryan said. "Some guys asked what we were doing, and we told them we were looking for a place to camp. They said they had the whole area. We asked what they were doing, and they said it was a religious retreat."

Chris nodded but said nothing.

"I guess it's good to know where they are," Rand said.

"There's a two-week limit on camping in the area," Caleb said.

"I don't know how well that's enforced," Ryan added.

Chris shrugged. "They can do whatever they like," she said. "I really don't care."

"Time to get back to work," Sheri called, and they moved back to their places.

Chris leaned toward Rand again. "There may be a two-week camping limit, but they aren't going to leave until they have me," she said.

"They will if we persuade them that they're wasting their time," he said.

She pressed her lips together and shook her head, but

she said nothing else as the lights dimmed and Sheri resumed her lecture.

At evening's end, they stayed to rearrange chairs and clean up. Danny found Rand carting the coffee urn into the tiny galley. "Did I tell you that one of your jobs as medical adviser is to help update our treatment protocols?"

"Sure, I can do that." Rand set the urn on the counter. "Any particular protocols?"

Danny made a face. "It's been a while since any of them were reviewed. Could you meet one day next week to go over them?"

"I'm off on Tuesday. Would that work?"

"That would be great." He glanced over his shoulder, then turned back, his voice lower. "I saw you sticking pretty close to Chris. Is she okay?"

"I'm fine." She moved in behind them with a handful of paper plates. She shoved the plates into the trash and faced Danny. "If you want to know how I'm doing, ask me."

"Sorry." He held up both hands. "But if you need anything—anything at all—you can call on any member of the team. We're not just about saving tourists, you know."

Her expression softened. "Thanks. That means a lot."

They exited the building and started across the parking lot, only to be hailed by Bethany. "I work at Peak Jeep Tours," she said. "Stop by if you're ever in the neighborhood. I'd really like to know you better."

"Um, sure." Chris hurried away, and Rand sped up to keep pace with her.

"Why is she so interested in me?" Chris asked when he caught up with her.

"I think she's just friendly."

"I'm not used to other people focusing on me—or caring so much," Chris said when she and Rand were in his car, headed back toward her apartment. "It feels a little uncomfortable."

"*Uncomfortable* but not *bad*, right?"

"Yeah."

"Can I ask you a personal question?"

"You can ask. That doesn't mean I'll answer."

"Fair enough. The blue hair and the tattoos—is that a fashion choice or another way of disguising yourself?"

She didn't say anything for so long he thought he might have offended her. But he had learned early in his medical career about the value of giving people plenty of time to answer hard questions. "A little of both, I think," she said. "My mother dyed my hair the day we escaped the camp, and I kept changing it over the years so I would look unfamiliar to anyone who knew me before. As for the tattoos—" she held out her arm "—we were taught that religious offerings were supposed to be perfect. Unblemished. I think in the back of my head I thought the Exalted would view a tattoo as an imperfection. That's why I got the first one, but after that, I liked it. It was another artistic expression." She shifted in the seat. "Why do you ask?"

"Just curious. They seem to suit you."

He pulled up to the door at the back of her building this time and met her beneath the light, waiting while she unlocked the outside entrance. They mounted the stairs side by side. She glanced down at his hand tensed at his side, as if reaching for something. "Are you carrying a gun?" she asked.

"Yes." He pulled up his shirt enough to show a holstered pistol. "I was in the military for years. I got used to walking around armed."

She nodded and they continued to her door. Once there, she turned to face him. "Look, I appreciate your concern. I really do. But these people are unpredictable. They seem nice and normal, until they aren't."

"I know that already. Remember, I've dealt with a cult before. They reel people in by appearing perfectly sensible and smarter than everyone else."

"Right. It's just…if something goes wrong, don't blame yourself, okay? You're not responsible for me. I'm not your sister."

Her expression was so earnest, her dark eyes so full of concern. As if she was more worried about him than about herself. His gaze shifted to her lips, full and slightly parted. "I don't feel about you like I do my sister." The words emerged more gruffly than he had planned. Then he yielded to temptation and kissed her.

For a fraction of a breath, she became a statue once his lips were on hers, unmoving. Not breathing. Then she pressed one hand to his chest, fingers slightly curled, seeking purchase. She arched into him, returning the kiss. He cupped his hand to her cheek, her skin hot, as if blushing at his touch. With a breathy moan, her lips parted, and she pressed against him, fitted to him, supple and strong. He wrapped both arms around her, cradling her to him yet holding back, his feelings so intense he feared crushing her.

She broke the kiss and stared up at him, a dazed expression in her eyes. "You'd better go," she whispered.

He wanted to argue but didn't. Instead, he reluctantly released his hold and waited while she unlocked her door and disappeared inside. He heard the dead bolt engage, then turned and moved away, down the stairs and into the darkness. So much of him was still there on that landing, wrapped up in that unexpected kiss.

He didn't see the person who came up behind him, only felt his presence and started to turn; then something hard crashed into his head, driving him to his knees. "Chris!" he tried to shout, but the word came out as a murmur as darkness swallowed him.

Chapter Seven

Chris sank onto the sofa, head back, eyes closed. That kiss! She hadn't even realized she was interested in Rand that way—that climb-his-body, take-me-now, where-have-you-been-all-my-life, passion-turned-up-to-ten kind of way—and then she was. When had she ever been kissed like that? Never. She had *never* been kissed like that. She didn't let men get that close. But Rand had vaulted right over her defenses and ambushed her with that kiss.

And she had willingly surrendered. Except it hadn't felt like losing—it felt like winning a grand prize. The rush of victory was overwhelming. It had been all she could do to pull herself together enough to send him away. At least she had that much of a sense of self-preservation left. After years of caution, she wasn't going to leap off that cliff just yet.

Harley climbed up onto the sofa beside her and began licking her cheek. She opened her eyes and hugged the dog. "I'm okay," she said. "Everything's okay."

Whomp!

The sound jolted her upright. Harley barked loudly, the ridge of hair along his back at attention. Something heavy had hit her door. It came again, an impact that made the door rattle in its frame. Heart pounding painfully, she jumped up, scrambling to free her phone from her pocket. A third impact shook the door, and Harley's barking became more frantic.

She stabbed at the phone as she moved toward the back door. "Nine-one-one. What is your emergency?"

"Someone is breaking into my apartment." She reached the kitchen just as the glass in the door's small window shattered inward. "Please hurry!"

"What is your location, ma'am?"

Chris rattled off her address as she grabbed the chef's knife from the magnet by the stove. She looked around for anything else she could use as a weapon. The frying pan? A rolling pin? Then she spotted the fire extinguisher and pulled it from its bracket on the wall. "Come on, Harley," she called, and headed toward the bedroom. She heard the back door give way as she dove into the closet and shut the door behind her and the dog. They would find her soon enough, but she hoped she would be able to hold them off until help arrived.

RAND GROANED AND tried to sit, but a wave of dizziness dragged him down again. He was aware of noises—someone shouting, pounding footsteps. Then hands grabbed him roughly. He fought back, punching out, and tried to shout, but no words emerged. He tried to open his eyes yet saw nothing but blackness.

"Hey, it's okay. You're all right now. You're safe. Lie still." The voice was firm but reassuring. Strong hands urged him to lie back, and he surrendered to the pull of gravity. A bright light shone on his face, and he squinted against it. A man he didn't know peered down at him. "Who are you?" Rand managed to force out.

"I'm Lee. I'm a paramedic with Rayford County Emergency Services. Looks like you hit your head pretty hard. Can you tell me what happened?"

Rand closed his eyes again, trying to remember. "Someone jumped me," he said.

"Lie still, okay? You're still bleeding a little. Do you know who hit you?"

He was starting to think more clearly, and the memory of what had happened before he was hit came flooding back. "Chris!" He tried to sit up again, though the EMTs held him down. "Is Chris all right? I have to go to her."

"Is Chris the person who called for an ambulance?" Lee asked someone out of Rand's field of vision. He was still holding Rand down. Rand lay back, gathering strength for another attempt to rise.

"No. Someone named Susan, in the apartment across the alley," a female voice answered. "She said she heard a shout and looked out the window to see someone fall to the ground and someone else run away. She called 911, and they dispatched us." A woman with strawberry blond hair and freckles leaned over Rand. "A sheriff's deputy is on the way. I hear the siren now."

Rand heard it too—a high-pitched wailing that grew louder and louder. He sat up again. This time no one stopped him. The woman probed at the back of his head while Lee unwrapped a blood pressure cuff from around Rand's left arm.

"Your vitals are good," Lee said. "How are you feeling?"

The dizziness and nausea had subsided. His head throbbed, but he could live with that. "I'm better," he said. "I have to check on Chris. The person who hit me could have got to her."

Lee's forehead wrinkled. "This Chris person was with you when you were attacked?"

"No. She lives upstairs, over the art gallery. I was just leaving her apartment. Whoever hit me must have been waiting in the alley."

"If she's upstairs, she should be all—" A loud crash interrupted him. He turned to look toward the sound behind him, and Rand staggered to his feet.

"Sir, you need to be still—"

Rand ignored the words and started for the building. He was certain now that his attacker had been waiting to disable him so he could go after Chris. But he had taken only a few steps when a sheriff's department SUV turned into the alley. The wail of the siren bounced off the buildings, and Rand instinctively put his hands to his ears. "Freeze, with your hands where I can see them!" a voice from the SUV ordered.

Rand did as he was asked and squinted in the glare of the spotlight centered on him. Then the light cut off, and a man stepped out from the car. "Rand, what are you doing here?"

Jake Gwynn moved toward Rand, converging on him at the same time the two EMTs caught up with him. "You need to check on Chris," Rand said. "I had just left her apartment when someone attacked me, but I think their real target was her."

"Chris called 911 and said someone was breaking into her apartment." Jake looked at the outer door. "Gage is on his way."

"We don't have time to wait," Rand said. "I'll back you up."

Jake's gaze shifted to Rand's head. "You're bleeding."

"I'll be fine. We don't have time to loo—"

A woman's scream overhead launched him toward the door, with Jake right behind him. But the door was locked. Jake pounded on it. "Open up! Sheriff's department!" he shouted.

But the only reply was scuffling noises overhead and another loud crash. "Is there a back way in?" Jake asked.

"I don't know," Rand said. He tried to remember anything about Chris's apartment, but he hadn't been paying attention, and he hadn't been past the living room. "Maybe a fire escape?"

"Stay here. I'm going around back."

As soon as Jake was gone, Rand turned his attention back to the door. It was a heavy metal door; he doubted he could bash it in. He couldn't pick the lock either. Could he ram it with his car?

A second siren's wail filled the air. "That must be Gage," Lee said.

Rand moved to the middle of the alley and stared up at what he thought was Chris's window. "Chris!" he shouted. But no answer came.

A second black-and-white SUV entered the alley, and Sergeant Gage Walker stepped out almost before it had come to a complete stop. "What's going on?" he asked.

"Chris is upstairs," Rand said. "She called 911, saying someone was breaking into her apartment. I had just left her, and someone must have been waiting for me. They attacked me and knocked me out. I came to when the paramedics arrived."

"Dispatch sent us over in response to a call from a neighbor about a man being attacked in the alley," Lee said.

Gage pulled out his phone. "I'll call the building owner and see if we can get a key."

Rand shook his head and started around the corner of the building. Jake met him at the corner. "Where are you going?" he asked, his hands on Rand's shoulders.

"I'm going up the fire escape," Rand said. "I'm not waiting for a key."

"The stairs aren't down," Jake said. "No one's been up there."

"Or they've been up there and pulled the stairs up after them," Rand said. He pushed past Jake and headed toward the fire escape. As Jake had said, the bottom of the stairs was ten feet overhead, out of his reach.

Rand pulled out his phone and dialed Chris's number. It rang five times before going to voicemail. "I can't take your call right now…" He ended the call and shoved the phone back into his pocket. By this time, Jake had caught up with him. "She's not answering," Rand said. "I know something's wrong."

Gage called to them from the corner of the building. "The landlord is on the way," he said. "She said she'll be here in five minutes."

Rand looked up at the fire escape again. If he parked his SUV beneath it, he could climb on top and maybe reach the bottom of the ladder from there. He pulled his keys from his pocket. "Where are you going?" Jake asked.

"To help Chris." Waiting was only buying more time for her to end up hurt. Or worse.

CHRIS HEARD THE SIREN, growing louder by the second until the wailing was directly below. Then the sound shut off. Help was almost here. She just had to hang on a little longer.

The intruder was in the house now, footsteps lumbering as they—because it sounded like more than one person—

searched the apartment. Something heavy, a piece of furniture, fell to the floor with a crash. "We know you're in here, Elita!" a man—Jedediah?—called out.

Harley growled, a low and menacing rumble. Chris buried her fingers in the thick ruff at his neck. "Quiet!" she hissed. They needed to remain hidden until the deputies arrived. What was taking them so long?

The footsteps entered the bedroom. Chris's heart hammered. She let go of the dog and gripped the knife in her right hand, then thought better of that and slid it into her pocket. She hefted the fire extinguisher and looped her finger into the metal ring on the handle.

Crash! A scream escaped her as something hit the closet door, causing it to bow inward. Harley lunged at the door, barking furiously. Chris braced against the back wall of the closet and stood, shoving clothes aside and balancing the fire extinguisher on one thigh. Her pulse sounded so loud in her ear she could scarcely hear anything else, though the dog's barking echoed in the small space.

The door burst open, splinters flying. Chris pulled the ring from the handle of the fire extinguisher, aimed the hose and squeezed the trigger. She hit her intruder right in the face. When the second man shoved the first out of the way and lunged for her, she got him, too, white powder billowing up and coating his glasses and hair and filling his mouth when he opened it to shout.

When the extinguisher was empty, Chris swung it like a club. She hit the second man hard on the shoulder. When he staggered back, the first man rushed forward, and she thrust the bottom of the extinguisher into his forehead, connecting with a sickening *thwack*—like a hammer hitting a watermelon. The first man grabbed on to the door of the closet but remained standing, only to be driven farther back by Harley, who rushed forward, teeth bared.

"Freeze! Sheriff's department!" came a shout from the front room.

The first man turned; then the second grabbed his shoulder. "We better get out of here," he said. They raced from the room. Chris dropped the fire extinguisher and sank to her knees, arms wrapped around Harley, who was still barking and lunging.

That was how Jake Gwynn found her. She had to calm the dog before he could approach, but once she had convinced Harley that everything was okay, Jake helped her to the end of the bed, where she sat and contemplated the closet's shattered door and the carpeting coated with white powder.

"There were two men," she said. "They broke in, and I hid in the closet with Harley. They ran when they heard you coming."

"Gage went after them," Jake said. "Do you know who they are?"

"Oh, I'm sure they were members of the Vine," she said. "They're the only ones who would want to hurt me. One of them might have been Jedediah."

"Did you get a good look at them?" Jake asked. "Could you identify them?"

She shook her head. "By the time I saw them, they were covered in the powder from the fire extinguisher." She closed her eyes, replaying those few split seconds. "And I think their faces were covered. They wore ski masks or something like that. And gloves." She had the image of black-gloved hands reaching for her fixed in her mind.

"Chris!"

Rand's cry made her sit up straighter. "We're in the bedroom," Jake called. "Don't come in. You could contaminate evidence." He indicated the footprints in the powder on the carpet, which he had avoided when he entered the room. "Those are from your attackers. We might be able to match them to their shoes later."

Rand appeared in the doorway. "Chris, are you all right?" he asked.

"I'm fine." She passed a shaky hand through her hair. "They never laid a hand on me."

Rand surveyed the chaos around the closet. "What happened?"

"She let off a fire extinguisher at them," Jake said, a note of admiration in his voice.

"I hit them with it too," she said. "And there's a kitchen knife in my pocket. I would have used it on them if I had to. And I had Harley." She hugged the dog, as much out of affection as to keep him from bounding across the powdered carpet to Rand.

"You shouldn't be in here, Rand," Jake said. "Go back outside and wait. Let the ambulance crew finish looking you over."

"Ambulance?" Chris turned to Rand. "Are you hurt? What happened?"

He touched the back of his head and winced. "Whoever went after you was waiting for me. They knocked me out, but I'm fine. Just a bump on the head."

Gage moved in behind him. "They got away down the fire escape," he said. "I didn't even get a good look at them. Two men dressed in black, covered in flour or something."

"Most of the contents of a fire extinguisher," Jake said. "Chris let them have it when they came after her."

"Good thinking." Gage studied the footprints on the floor. "I'll call for a forensics team. Are you all right, Chris? Do you need the paramedics?"

"I'm okay," she said.

"We'll need to get your statement," Gage said. "Jake, bring her in the other room." He turned to Rand. "We'll need your statement too."

Jake directed her in picking her way around the path the intruders had taken when they fled the apartment. She guided Harley, who wasn't in a cooperative mood, out of the apartment and down the stairs, where she found two patrol vehicles, an ambulance, two paramedics, her landlord and half a dozen curious onlookers.

Rand moved in beside her. "Are you sure you're okay?" he asked, his gaze taking her in from the top of her head to her feet.

She nodded and hugged her arms across her chest, having released Harley to sniff around, knowing the dog wouldn't go far. "I was terrified for a few minutes. Now I'm just exhausted."

Her landlord, Jasmine, approached. With no makeup on and wearing a sweatshirt pulled over plaid pajama pants, she looked very different from the polished professional Chris was used to. "Honey, are you okay?" Jasmine asked.

"I'm fine. I'm sorry about the apartment doors." She looked at the doors, both bent inward.

"The cops did that," Jasmine said. "I guess they couldn't wait for me to get here with the key."

Chris shuddered. "They got to me just in time."

"Who cares about doors, as long as you're okay." Jasmine patted her arm. "Don't worry about it. I have insurance. But is there anything else you need?"

"No, thanks. I'm okay, really."

"Your friend here looks a little worse for wear." Jasmine flashed a smile. "Still very easy on the eyes, mind you."

Chris studied Rand. His face was paler than usual, the fine lines around his eyes tighter, as if he was in pain. And was that blood in his hair?

"Rand, you're hurt!" she exclaimed.

"I'm okay. The paramedics have seen me."

"Jake, get Rand's statement," Gage said as he joined them. "Chris, you come with me."

She ended up sitting in the front seat of Gage's patrol car, reciting all the events of the evening, leaving out the part about her and Rand kissing before he left her and returned to his car. "I'm sure those two men were from the Vine," she said. "The group has made it clear they want me back."

"To marry their leader—have I got that right?" Gage asked.

She nodded. "It sounds ridiculous. I'm a grown woman. I'm not a member of the group anymore. They can't force me to marry someone. Especially since he's already married to someone else. But logic doesn't really matter. They think they can make me do this. And they believe they're above the law."

"Did the two men who broke into your apartment say anything?" Gage asked.

"One of them called me Elita," she said. "That was the name I used when I was a member of the group—when I was a little girl. That's one more reason I'm sure they were from the Vine. No one else knows me by that name."

Gage made a note. "Anything else you remember about them?"

"I thought the voice sounded like Jedediah. He's the man

who confronted me at the fire the other day. I had seen him on a hiking trail the day before that, when search and rescue responded to a man on the Anderson Falls Trail who had heart trouble."

"We'll have forensics go over the place," Gage said. "You won't be able to stay here for a while. The front and back doors to your apartment were forced open."

"How did they get in from street level?" she asked.

"Best guess is they blocked the door from closing all the way while you and Rand were upstairs. He came down, and they ambushed him at his car, then went in the door and locked it behind them to delay anyone's ability to get to them."

"And to slow me down if I managed to run from them," she said.

"We had to break open the outer door to get to you," Gage said. "I was going to wait for Jasmine to bring us the key, but Rand insisted. I guess it's a good thing he did."

She said nothing, feeling Gage's eyes on her. She wondered what he thought of the tattoos and dyed hair. Of her strange past with a cult that seemed kooky to most people. "Have they threatened you before?" he asked. "Since you left?"

"Mom and I were approached a couple of times by members who recognized us." She shivered, remembering. "No direct threats. I think they're too clever for that. But if you had lived with them the way we did, you'd know how things that sound innocent can come across as really menacing."

"Give me an example."

She shifted in her seat, then blew out a breath. Why was this so hard to talk about? "If someone approached you and said, 'The Exalted is worried it will be really bad for you if you don't fulfill your destiny,' that sounds innocent enough, right? A little out there, but harmless. But when I hear that, I'm not thinking they're concerned about my karma or my mental health or even the threat of eternal damnation—I'm hearing code for 'If you don't do what we want, you could end up dead.'"

"Did that happen to other people who disobeyed the Exalted?" Gage asked.

"Oh yeah. No one ever used the word *murder.* They got sick. They had an accident. One young woman drowned."

"Were any of these deaths investigated by law enforcement?"

She shook her head. "They weren't even reported, as far as I know. The victims were buried in the woods, wherever we were staying. That was the way we did things. Everyone said, 'We take care of our own,' and it was considered a good thing. We didn't need outsiders interfering."

Gage closed his notebook. "I'll probably have more questions later. Do you have some place you can stay? Or I can find you a bed at a women's shelter."

"I'll find a place." She could always go to her mother's, though the idea left a sour taste in her mouth. Hadn't she said she was tired of running away? And what about bringing the danger with her?

At a tapping on the glass, she turned and saw Rand outside the SUV. Gage rolled down the window. "You can't stay here," Rand said. "Come back to my place. No one from the Vine knows where I live."

"Rand, you're hurt," she said. "You should have someone look at your head. You might need an X-ray or stitches."

"I'm fine. I have a headache, but no dizziness. The bleeding has stopped. I know enough to go to the hospital if any concerning symptoms pop up. In the meantime, these people don't know where I live, and I have a good security system. You'll be safe there."

"I told her I could find her a bed in a women's shelter," Gage said. "The local animal shelter would look after your dog for you."

She didn't want to go to a shelter, and she wasn't going to leave Harley. "Can Harley come to your place?" she asked Rand.

"Of course." He opened the door. The dog was standing next to him. "He's ready to go."

Chapter Eight

Gage fetched a list of items Chris needed from her apartment, and Rand loaded them into his SUV before they headed out. No one said much. He didn't try to reassure her that everything would be all right or offer advice for how she should act or feel. She was grateful for that. She laid her head back and closed her eyes, the dark silence and the rhythm of the vehicle's tires on the road almost lulling her to sleep.

But not quite. The fear was still there, coiled inside her, waiting to spring to life. That fear made her open her eyes again and repeatedly check the side mirror, looking out for headlights coming up behind them.

"No one is following us," Rand said. "I've been watching."

"I'm sorry I pulled you into this," she said. This was why she didn't get close to people. She didn't want anyone to see the mess of her life. It was like having an acquaintance rifle through the contents of your kitchen garbage can or your dirty-clothes hamper.

"I want to help." He glanced at her, then back at the road. "Just to be clear, this invitation to stay with me comes with no strings attached."

Was he thinking of that kiss? The memory pulled at her, here in the dark, so close to him. Yet everything that happened afterward was a barrier between them now. "Thanks," she said. "I like you. I guess that's pretty clear from that kiss. But... I have a lot to process right now. And I'm not used to trusting other people."

"Fair enough. Just know you can trust me."

She wanted to believe that, but she had had so little practice in depending on other people. She thought of all the rescue calls she had been on, when strangers trusted her and her fellow volunteers to save them. Those people, injured or stranded in the wilderness, didn't have much choice in the matter. Maybe she didn't have much choice either. She wasn't strong enough to fight the Vine on her own. She believed Rand was strong, and she believed he really did want to help her. That was more than anyone else had given her, which made it a good place to start.

RAND'S HOME HAD once been a summer camp. He had purchased the long-abandoned property, torn down the dilapidated camper cabins and turned the log structure that had served as a lodge into a home. The remote location—the only property at the end of a long gravel road—had added to the hassle of the remodel, but now he appreciated the privacy and the safety it would offer Chris.

"The guest room and bath are upstairs," he told her as she and Harley followed him into the great room that made up most of the ground floor. "The primary suite is down here, so you'll have plenty of privacy." He led the way up the stairs to the guest room. "I use the room across the hall as my home office. Kitchen and laundry are downstairs, and there's a detached garage in back. There's an alarm system and a sensor on the driveway that will alert me if anyone tries to drive in."

"Is there something you need to tell me, Doctor?" she asked. "Some reason for all this security?"

"Let's just say I'm a naturally cautious person."

Harley sat beside her and leaned on her leg. She rubbed the dog's ears and looked into the bedroom but didn't go in. "Thank you," she said. "I couldn't ask for a better setup."

"You're welcome to stay as long as you like. I work three or four ten- to twelve-hour shifts per week at the hospital, so you'll be alone during that time. I hope that's not a problem."

"No. I'm used to being by myself." She entered the room, trailed by the dog, then looked back at him. "Good night," she said, and closed the door.

She had spoken so matter-of-factly about being accustomed to being alone, but her words made him feel a little hollow. He would have answered the same way and protested that he liked his own company. But there had been times when he had wished for companionship to fill that emptiness. He hoped he could be that for her.

Five years ago

"SOMEONE FROM THE VINE was here tonight."

Chris's mom sounded calm on the phone, but her words sent an icy shard of fear through Chris. "They came to your house? You spoke to them?"

"It was a man and a woman. They were waiting on the front steps when I came in from work. They were in the shadows, so I didn't see them until I was almost to the door. They were dressed in suits and carrying a big Bible, like missionaries going door-to-door. But when I told them I wasn't interested and tried to move past them, the man grabbed me."

Chris sucked in her breath. "Mom! Did they hurt you?"

"They only frightened me. But that was what they intended."

"What did they say? What did they do?"

"They forced their way into the house and kept asking me where you were. They said the Exalted was ready to marry you and it was time for you to fulfill your destiny."

"I thought they would have forgotten me by now," Chris said. "That the Exalted would have found someone else to marry." After all this time, she still thought of him by that title. His given name—Edmund Harrison—felt too strange on her tongue.

"I promise I didn't tell them where you are," her mother said. "But they said to tell you they weren't going to give up looking for you. And they said…they said…" Her voice broke.

Chris took a deep breath, trying to stop the shaking that had taken over her body but failing. "What did they say?"

"They said if you won't come back to them, you're dead to them. And they'll make sure you're dead to everyone else too."

"They're going to kill me just because I won't come back to their cult and marry a man who's old enough to be my father and already has at least one wife?" The idea was absurd, yet Chris didn't have it in her to laugh. She still remembered how seriously the members of the group took the Exalted's every pronouncement.

"They killed your father," her mother said. "And I'm sure they've killed other people. Eliminating anyone who gets out of line is one way the Exalted keeps order."

"You defied them by taking me away," Chris said. "Did they threaten you too?"

"They said…if you didn't obey, they would find a way to hurt me."

"No." A wave of nausea rocked Chris, but she pulled herself together, allowing anger to overcome the sickness. "That's not going to happen."

"I'm packing my things already. And I have my extra ID." Back when they had first left the group, her mother had paid for new birth certificates and Social Security cards for the two of them. Later, she had paid even more for a second set of identification. Chris kept hers in a lockbox under her bed, but she hadn't even looked at the papers for years.

"I'm coming to get you," Chris said. "I'll help you move."

"No! They're probably watching me, and they'll see you. I have a friend who will help me. He's a former cop. He knows a little of my story. I trust him. I'll be in touch with my new information when it's safe to do so."

"What about going to the police?" Chris asked. "If we tell them about these threats…"

"There's nothing they can do," her mother said. "The Exalted can produce witnesses all day long to attest to his sterling character. He has money and powerful friends to protect him. We don't have any proof they've threatened us."

"We know they've killed people," Chris said.

"But we can't prove it. Better to start over with a new name. I'm getting used to it now."

Gloom settled over Chris. "Do you think I should move and change my name too?"

"No, no! They don't know where you are. If they did, they wouldn't have wasted their time with me. There's no need for you to worry. I wouldn't even have bothered you with this, except I wanted you to know I'll be unreachable for a few days. Just until I get resettled."

"Of course I'm worried, Mom! What if they come after you again?"

"They won't. I've gotten very good at covering my tracks. I'm going to hang up now, sweetie. Love you. Talk to you soon. Oh, and next time we talk, remember—my new name is April."

Chris hung up the phone and slumped onto the sofa, stomach churning. Her mother hadn't sounded scared or even terribly upset. The two of them had moved five times between Chris's twelfth and eighteenth birthdays, and her mother had relocated twice more since Chris had left home. After all these years of running and hiding, Chris sometimes thought her mother enjoyed the challenge and the chance to start over and remake herself once again.

Whereas all Chris had ever wanted was to sink roots in one place, to be part of a community. She had found that here in Eagle Mountain. She had artist friends and her search and rescue friends and people whom she believed cared about her. Though she wasn't particularly close to any single person, she felt comfortable with them all. The thought of having to leave that behind was too heavy a burden to carry.

And all because one evil man was fixated on her. The Exalted had been getting his way for so long he couldn't bear the thought of anyone denying him—even a child, as she had been when she ran away from him. She wanted the running and hiding to stop, but she didn't know how to make it happen.

She still remembered her father, lying on the bed in their little trailer, writhing in agony. This was what the Exalted's punishment looked like. If the Vine ever caught up with her, they would make sure she obeyed, or they would mete out a similar fate. She was as sure of that as she had once been certain of the other teachings she had learned as a little girl. She had left those other false beliefs behind, but watching her father die had sealed this one certainty within her. She couldn't risk the Exalted catching up with her, so she had to keep running.

BEFORE CHRIS EVEN opened her eyes the next morning, she had the dreamlike sensation of being in an unfamiliar place. She opened her eyes to a shadowed bedroom, a thin comforter over the top of the bed, Harley stretched out along her side. No dream, then. She was in the guest room in Rand's home. For a few seconds the terror of those moments in the closet, hearing heavy footsteps approach her hiding place, threatened to overwhelm her. She rested a hand on the dog, feeling his side rise and fall, and grew calmer. She was safe. No one was going to hurt her.

She sat up and looked around the plain but comfortable guest room. Moving around so much, she was used to being in unfamiliar places, but almost always alone or with her mother. Not in a house belonging to a man she really liked but wasn't sure she should be with.

She got up and got ready for the day. Dressed in jeans and a T-shirt, she went downstairs to let Harley out. The rooms were empty, Rand's SUV no longer parked out front. While Harley patrolled the property, she hunted in the kitchen for coffee and started it brewing. Rand had left a note on the kitchen table with a set of car keys.

My shift is 6–4 today. The keys are to the Jeep in the garage. Feel free to use it. Help yourself to anything you like. Text if you need anything. Rand

Harley scratched at the door, and after making sure the noise really was from the dog, she let him in, then carried a cup of coffee upstairs and started the shower.

After she and the dog both had breakfast, she wandered the house. Rand had a few decent pieces of art on the walls—a mix of photos and original oils or watercolors, some from local artists she knew. His bookshelves housed medical texts, historical nonfiction and detective stories. One photo showed him standing with an older man and woman, the man an older version of Rand himself. *So these must be his parents.* No photo of his sister. Maybe that reminder would be too painful.

She avoided his bedroom. She was nosy, but she wasn't going to be that intrusive. House tour over, she returned to her room and made her bed but was unable to settle. She needed something to focus on besides the Vine. Usually, she could lose herself in her art, but she didn't have any supplies.

"Want to go for a ride, Harley?"

The dog wagged his tail and trotted ahead of her down the stairs. She collected the keys from the kitchen table and headed for the garage. Nice that Rand had a spare vehicle. One the Vine wouldn't recognize as hers.

At the last minute, she texted him. If he came home before she returned, she didn't want him to think the worst. Plus, her work with search and rescue had ingrained in her the advice that when setting out alone on a risky activity like a hike or skiing, it was smart to let someone know your plans. Running errands in town shouldn't be risky, but considering her situation, it might be.

Decided to run a few errands in town. Back soon.

He responded with a thumbs-up emoji. She smiled. Odd

how that made her feel better. She headed toward her apartment, almost without thinking. But she didn't park in back. Instead, she pulled the Jeep into a parking spot right in front of the gallery and sat for a few minutes, observing passers-by. No one looked like anyone from the Vine. Over the years she had gotten good at spotting them, with their slightly outdated fashion and simple hairstyles; the men always clean shaven, the women without makeup. Even more important, no one was paying particular attention to the building or to her.

Harley waited on the sidewalk while Chris went inside the gallery. The bell on the door sounded, and Jasmine bustled out of the workroom in the back. She stopped short when she recognized Chris. Today the frames of her glasses were red, matching the large red stones in her earrings. "Chris, how are you?" she asked, then hurried over to give her a hug.

Chris patted Jasmine awkwardly on the back and stepped out of her embrace. "I'm fine."

Jasmine nodded. "You look better. Not so pale. What happened last night was horrible. Do you have any idea who would do such a thing?"

"None," she lied. "I stopped by to pick up some supplies."

She had hoped to change the subject, but Jasmine didn't take the hint. "I've got someone coming tomorrow to see about replacing the doors on your apartment," she said. "But you're going to have a major mess to clean up. The sheriff's department left fingerprint dust, or whatever you call it, everywhere."

"Don't worry about that," Chris said. "I'll take care of it. And I'll reimburse you for the doors."

Jasmine shook her head. "I told you, my insurance will

take care of that. But what happened? The sheriff's deputy didn't say much, just that someone tried to break in."

"I think they had me confused with someone else," she lied again. She didn't want to go into the whole backstory. The circumstances would probably make Jasmine think twice about renting to her. "I just came in for a few things, then I'll be out of your way." In addition to the artwork for sale, Jasmine stocked a small selection of canvases, paints, pastels, sketchbooks and other supplies.

"Oh, honey, you're no trouble. You're the best tenant I ever had. Most of the time I wouldn't even know you're up there, you're so quiet." Jasmine followed her over to the corner devoted to supplies. "Deputy Gwynn said there were two guys who tried to break in, but they got away. He told me to keep an eye out for anyone hanging around the store, but I haven't seen anyone. Did you get a good look at them? Do you know who they are?"

"I only had a brief glimpse of them." Chris selected a sketchbook and pencils. "It was dark, and they were wearing ski masks."

"It's just the wildest thing. I mean, you don't think about something like that happening here. I hope they don't come back. They might think there's money in the gallery, though I make it a point not to leave much cash on hand, and I wouldn't think artwork was something they could readily sell."

"I'm sure the sheriff's deputies scared them off." Chris added an art gum eraser to her purchases. "I'll take these."

"Where are you staying?" Jasmine asked as she rang up Chris's selections.

"With a friend," she said. She didn't wait for Jasmine to probe for more details, instead collecting the art supplies and her change and starting for the door. "I have to run. See you soon."

She decided to walk over to the bank and get some cash. She hadn't gone very far when someone called her name. "Chris!"

She turned to see Bethany Ames hurrying toward her. As usual, Bethany was smiling. "I'm glad I ran into you," Bethany said. "I came into town to grab some lunch. We could eat together."

Chris had already taken a step back. "I don't really have time right now. Thanks anyway."

Bethany's smile faded. "If you don't want to hang out with me, you can be honest. It's because I made such a fool of myself with Vince, isn't it?" She covered her eyes with her hand. "I'm never going to live that down. But honest, I didn't know he was involved with someone else. I'm new here in town, right? I'm trying to make friends—to be more outgoing and positive. That's what you're supposed to do, isn't it? But I keep getting it wrong. I'm sorry to bother you." She turned away.

"Wait," Chris called. Bethany's raw honesty was shocking, and also appealing. And Chris knew a little about being the "new kid" and trying to find a way to fit in. "I'll have lunch with you. What's this about you and Vince?" Vince Shepherd was a fellow search and rescue volunteer who was living with *Eagle Mountain Examiner* reporter Tammy Patterson.

"Are you sure?" Bethany asked. "I don't want to impose if you're busy."

"I have time," Chris said. "And I want to hear your story."

Bethany's smile returned. "In that case, I'm happy to give you the whole sad tale of me making a fool of myself.

I thought Vince was so good looking and I would sweep him off his feet with my awkward but endearing charm." She rolled her eyes. "Unfortunately—or maybe *fortunately*, since he already had a girlfriend—he was immune to my flirting. When I found out he was involved with someone else, I was mortified. I figured everyone in search and rescue knew about my crush on him."

"I didn't know," Chris said. "But then, I'm not usually clued in on local gossip." She wasn't close enough to other people for them to confide in her.

But Bethany was willing to tell all. She obviously needed someone to talk to, so why couldn't Chris be that person? The thought surprised her. Six months ago that wasn't something that would have occurred to her. She had always believed she didn't need close friends.

But Rand had refused to be put off by her reserve. Apparently, Bethany felt the same way. Chris smiled at her. "Let's go over to the Cake Walk and have lunch. You can tell me how you ended up in Eagle Mountain."

"It's a doozy of a story, I promise," Bethany said.

An hour later, Chris had shared a cheeseburger with Harley on the patio of the Cake Walk Café and learned all about Bethany, her three overprotective brothers and the fiancé who had jilted her. Despite what some would have labeled a tragedy, the young woman remained sunny and optimistic, and excited about starting life over alone in a new place, despite some bumps in the road along the way. Chris could never see herself being so upbeat, but spending time with her new friend had inspired her to do a better job of not dwelling on the hurts of her past. Bethany's approach to moving on struck her as healthier, though she suspected a lot of determination lay beneath the young woman's cheerful exterior.

She ended her afternoon in town at the local grocery, for a few items to add to Rand's supplies. She hesitated in front of a display of portobello mushrooms. She had a recipe for grilled mushrooms that Rand might like. She could make dinner for the two of them.

And then what? Would that be too much like a date? A chance to repeat that kiss and see if it had been a fluke or as sensational as she remembered?

She shook her head. "Don't get ahead of yourself," she mumbled, but she put the mushrooms in her cart anyway.

She saw no one suspicious in town, and no one followed her back to Rand's place. She texted to let him know she had returned safely, but got no reply. Maybe he was in surgery.

She settled into a chair on the back deck and began to sketch the scene before her—a patch of woods, with mountains in the distance. Soon she was lost in the work. This was what she needed, what had always made her feel better—to let her unsettling thoughts find their way out through her pencil, transformed from fears to fantasies of a hidden world that she controlled.

RAND WAS HALFWAY home after his shift when he remembered he was supposed to meet Danny to review the medical protocols for search and rescue. He was tempted to call and cancel, but he resisted the urge and drove to SAR headquarters. Once there, he texted Chris to let her know he would be a little late. Should be done by 6:30 he said, and hit send before he could talk himself out of it. Had he assumed too much? It wasn't as if they were in a relationship and needed to report their comings and goings to each other. But he also didn't want to worry her when she already had so much to deal with.

Danny was waiting for him inside the building. "These are all our protocols," he said, hefting a large notebook. "Some of them are on the computer, too, but not all of them. Maybe eventually that will happen, but for now, we're still doing things the old-fashioned way."

"No problem," Rand said. "Let's see how many we can get through this afternoon."

They moved to a couple of folding chairs set up at a table near the front of the room. "I guess you heard about the commotion at Chris's last night," Danny said.

"You know about that?" Rand tried not to show his surprise.

Danny shrugged. "It's all over town. I guess people saw the sheriff's deputies there this morning."

"I did hear about it," Rand said, unsure how much to reveal. Should he mention that Chris was staying with him? He decided against it. Not that he didn't trust Danny, but it seemed safer for as few people as possible to know her whereabouts.

"I wonder if it was a random break-in or if someone targeted Chris," Danny said.

The comment surprised him. "Why would you think someone would target her?"

Danny shrugged. "She's pretty striking looking. Maybe she caught the wrong guy's attention. And for all she's been part of the group for four years, I don't know much about her. She's not one to talk much about herself. Which I respect, but most people aren't quite as, well, secretive as she is. And now there's this weird thing with some stranger declaring he's going to marry her?" He shook his head. "I just wonder if it's all connected."

Rand was sure the attack and Chris's past were connected, but would the sheriff be able to prove it? "Maybe the sheriff will find who did it," he said, and opened the notebook. "Let's get started on these protocols."

The work went quickly. The notebook was arranged alphabetically, with one to two sheets of paper outlining the proper treatment for each condition, from asthma attacks to wound care. Rand recommended a few updates and places where they might review their training. "Have you dealt with all of these conditions in the field?" he asked after he had studied the page for transient ischemic attack.

"Most of them," Danny said. "I've seen everything from third-degree burns from a campfire to heat exhaustion and broken bones. We've dealt with heart attacks, seizures and head injuries—if it can happen to someone when they're away from home, we might be called upon to treat it in the field, or at least stabilize the person until we can transport them to an ambulance."

"It looks to me like you're up to date on everything." Rand shut the notebook. "I'm impressed."

"Thanks," Danny said. "We try to run a professional organization, but when you rely on one hundred percent volunteers, things can fall through the cracks." He shoved back his chair. "Thanks again for your help."

Rand was about to tell him he was glad to be involved when hard pounding on the door made him flinch. He and Danny exchanged looks, then hurried toward the entrance, where the pounding continued. Danny opened the door. "What's going on?" he asked.

A twentysomething man with disheveled dark hair to his

shoulders and deep shadows beneath his eyes stood on the doorstep. He wore jeans faded to a soft shade of gray blue, an equally worn denim work shirt over a gray T-shirt and dirty straw sandals. "I need a doctor right away," he said.

"I'm a doctor." Rand stepped forward. "What's the problem?"

"It's not for me. It's for my sister." He clutched Rand's arm. "You have to come with me. Now."

"Let me call an ambulance." Danny pulled out his phone. "Where is your sister?"

"There isn't time for that," the man said. He struck out, sending Danny's phone flying.

"Hey!" Danny shouted.

"What's wrong with your sister?" Rand asked, trying to gain control of the situation.

"I think she's dying. You have to help her."

"An ambulance will help her more than I can," Rand said.

"No ambulance!" The man let go of Rand and stepped back. Rand thought he might leave, but instead, he pulled a pistol from beneath his shirt and pointed it at Rand. The end of the barrel was less than two feet from Rand's stomach. One twitch of the man's finger would inflict a wound Rand doubted he would survive. "Come with me now," the man ordered.

Chapter Nine

"Killing him won't save your sister," Danny said. Rand could see him out of the corner of his eye, his face as white as milk, the muscle beside his left eye twitching. But he kept his cool and spoke firmly.

"Don't think I won't shoot," the young man said. He shifted the pistol's aim to Danny. "You come too. You can help him."

"All right," Rand said. "We'll come with you." They'd look for an opportunity to overpower the young man. The odds were in their favor—two against one.

Still holding the gun, the man urged them toward a mostly powder blue sedan, which had been manufactured sometime in the 1980s, by Rand's best guess. As they approached, a second, larger man got out of the passenger seat and frowned at them. He was older than the first man but dressed similarly, his shirt a faded blue-and-white-checkered flannel; his shoes old house slippers, the suede worn shiny at the toes. He opened the back door, and Danny, with another wary glance at the gun, got in.

"You sit up front," the bigger man told Rand before joining Danny in the back seat. His voice was a reedy tenor, nasal and thin.

So much for two against one. Rand wondered if the second man was also armed, then decided he didn't want to find out. Instead, he focused on the driver, who shifted into gear with one hand, the other still holding the gun. "What's wrong with your sister?" he asked.

"She's having a baby," he said. "But something isn't right."

"What isn't right?"

"She's been in labor a long time, but nothing is happening."

"How long?"

The younger man hunched over the steering wheel, the barrel of the gun balanced on top. "Two days. A little longer."

"How advanced is her pregnancy?" Rand asked. "Has she lost much blood? How is the baby presented?"

"I don't know! Stop asking questions. You'll find out everything when you see her."

"Where are you taking us?" Danny asked.

"You'll find that out soon enough too."

Rand was aware of his phone in the back pocket of his jeans. Could he get his hand back there and dial 911? He shifted and slowly moved his hand back.

A meaty fist wrapped around his bicep. "I'll take the phone," the bigger man said.

When Rand didn't respond, the man squeezed harder, a jolt of pain traveling to the tips of Rand's fingers. Reluctantly, he surrendered the phone.

The car turned away from town and down a county road, which, after a couple of miles, narrowed and became an unpaved forest service road. Realization washed over Rand. "You're with the Vine, aren't you?" he asked.

"Who told you that?" the man from the back seat asked. He had released his hold on Rand but sat forward, within easy striking distance.

"I heard you had moved your camp to the woods," Rand said. He studied the driver more closely. Were these two the ones who had attacked him and Chris last night? Nothing about them looked familiar, but Rand hadn't gotten a look at whoever had hit him in the darkness.

Another turn onto an even narrower dirt lane brought them to a cluster of trailers and tents parked among the trees—everything from a battered Airstream to a truck camper up on blocks, old canvas tents, new nylon structures and even a large tepee. The driver stopped the car, and his companion got out and took hold of Rand's arm. "This way," he said.

People emerged from the various dwellings to stare as the two men led Danny and Rand past—men and women, many young, none older than middle age. Rand counted eight children and a couple of teens among them.

The driver stopped at a set of wooden steps that led into the back of a box truck. A door had been cut into the back panel of the box. "My sister is in here," the driver said, and pulled open the door.

The first thing that struck Rand was the smell—body odor and urine, but above that, the slightly sour, metallic scent of blood. The aroma plunged him back to the battlefield, trying to tend to soldiers who were bleeding out. He blinked, letting his eyes adjust to the dimness. The only light in the windowless space emanated from an LED camping lantern suspended from the ceiling. The woman was lying on a pallet in the middle of the floor, dark hair spread out around a narrow face bleached as white as the pillowcase, the swell of her pregnant belly mounding the sheets. A girl knelt beside her, laying a damp cloth on the woman's forehead. The girl couldn't have been more than

nine or ten, with long dark hair and eyes that looked up at
Rand with desperate pleading.

Three other people—two women and a man—were gathered around the pallet. They studied Rand and Danny with
suspicion. "Who are they?" the man—blond and stocky,
with thinning hair—asked.

"He's a doctor." The driver nudged Rand. "Go on."

Rand knelt beside the pallet. The girl started to get up
and move, but Rand motioned her to stay. "It's all right,"
he said. "I might need your help." He wouldn't ordinarily
ask a child to assist him, but this girl seemed calmer and
more willing than the others in the room.

The woman on the pallet was so still that he thought
at first she might already be dead. He took her wrist and
tried to find a pulse. It was there. Weak and irregular. He
looked up at her brother. "I can examine her, but I can tell
you already, she needs an ambulance."

"Examine her. There must be something you can do,"
the driver said.

Danny knelt on the other side of the pallet "Is the baby's
father here?" he asked.

The others in the room exchanged a look Rand couldn't
interpret. "He isn't here," the stocky man said after a tense
moment.

"I'm going to examine her," Rand told Danny. "Help me
get her into position."

The woman was almost completely unresponsive, only
moaning slightly when Danny moved her legs. The girl
took the young woman's hand and held it. Rand used the
sheets to form a drape around her and examined the woman
and her unborn child as best he could. The situation wasn't
pretty. The woman had lost a lot of blood, and the child was

wedged firmly in her narrow pelvis. Without a stethoscope, he couldn't tell if the child was even alive.

He covered the woman again and stood. "Whoever is responsible for leaving her in this state and not calling for help should be shot," he said. "I think the baby is dead, and she will be, too, soon, unless you call an ambulance."

"No ambulance," the stocky man said.

The door opened, bringing in a rush of fresh air. The others in the truck rose to their feet or, if already standing, stood up straighter. Rand turned to see Jedediah moving toward him, followed by several other men and women, some of whom Rand remembered from the day of the fire.

"Thank you for coming," the woman's brother said to Jedediah. He sounded close to tears.

"I've come as an emissary from the Exalted," Jedediah said. He looked down at the woman, who now moaned almost continuously and moved her head from side to side, eyes closed. "He is sorry to hear our sister is troubled."

"She's not troubled. She's going to die if you don't get her to a hospital right away," Rand said. She would probably still die, he thought. But at least in a medical facility, she had a chance.

"Silence!" Jedediah clamped down on Rand's shoulder, fingers digging in painfully. Rand shook him off. If the man touched him again, he would fight back.

Jedediah held up a palm, and everyone fell silent. He knelt and took the woman's hand in his own. "Sister, the Exalted sends his strength to you," he said. "Strength to deliver this child. You need not rely on your own frailties, but on his power."

The others in the room murmured some kind of affirmation. Rand looked on in disgust. Danny didn't look any happier than he did. Jedediah stood and turned to Rand. He smiled and stared into Rand's eyes with an expression Rand read as a threat. "I'm confident you can heal her," Jedediah said. "Tell us what you need, and we will bring it to you."

"She needs to be in the hospital."

"We don't need a hospital. We take care of our own. It's up to you to help her."

CHRIS TIMED DINNER to be ready at seven. When Rand still hadn't shown up, she turned off the heat under the mushrooms and told herself he had probably gotten involved in something at SAR headquarters. By seven thirty, she debated texting him, but she decided that would be out of line. He didn't owe her any explanations for how he spent his time. She fixed a plate for herself and set aside the leftovers to reheat when he came in.

By nine o'clock, she was truly worried. Rand hadn't struck her as the type to disappear without letting her know what was going on. She texted him Everything OK?

No reply. She stared at the phone screen. He had said he was meeting Danny, right? She sent a quick text to Danny. Is Rand with you?

No reply. A chill shuddered through her, even as she tried to tell herself there was a logical explanation for the failure of both men to reply. Maybe they had decided to go out after finishing up at headquarters, and time had gotten away from them. She hesitated, then looked up the number for Carrie Andrews, Danny's partner and fellow search and rescue volunteer.

"Chris? What's up?" Carrie answered right away as if she had been waiting for a call.

"Is Danny there?" Chris asked.

"No. He was meeting Rand at SAR headquarters and was supposed to be back by seven or so. I've been trying to reach him, but he's not answering his phone."

Chris's stomach clenched. "I've been trying to reach Rand. He's not answering either."

"I was going to drive over to headquarters and see if their cars are in the parking lot," Carrie said. "But I can't get hold of my mom to watch the kids, and I don't want to upset them."

"I'll go over there," Chris said, already pocketing the Jeep keys.

"Let me know what you find."

Chris had never realized how isolated the search and rescue headquarters building was before. Almost as soon as she turned onto the road leading up to the building, she left behind the lights of houses. She gripped the steering wheel tightly and checked her mirrors every few seconds to see if she was being followed. Relief momentarily relaxed her when she turned into the parking lot and spotted Rand's and Danny's vehicles side by side near the door. They must have become so engrossed in their work they had lost track of time.

She parked and hurried to the door, Harley at her heels. The security light flickered on at their approach. She grasped the knob, but the door was locked. "Hey, open up in there!" she called, and pounded on the door. No answer. She tried phoning Rand again. No answer. Next, she punched in Danny's number. He wasn't answering, either, but she could hear a phone ringing somewhere just on the other side of the door.

The phone stopped ringing, and she heard the electronic

message telling her she had been redirected to a voice mailbox.

She ended the call, and almost immediately, her phone rang. Carrie's voice was thin with worry. "Are you there? Did you find them?"

"Their cars are here, but no one is answering my knock," Chris said.

"Something's happened to them," Carrie said. "I'm going to call the sheriff."

"Do that," Chris said. "Tell them I'll wait for them here." She ended the call. Maybe she and Carrie were overreacting, but she didn't think so. Something was wrong. The knowledge tightened her gut and made her cold all over.

She waited twenty minutes, she and Harley sitting in her car with the doors locked, phone in hand, willing Rand to call. When headlights illuminated the lot, she sat up straighter. The Rayford County Sheriff's Department SUV swung in behind her, and Deputy Ryker Vernon got out. Chris went to meet him. "Hello, Chris," he said. "What's going on?"

"Rand Martin and Danny Irwin were supposed to meet here this afternoon about five o'clock," she said. "Their vehicles are here, but the door is locked and no one is answering my knock or my calls."

"What makes you think they didn't just go off with friends for a drink or something?" Ryker asked.

"Carrie was expecting Danny home. The last time I spoke with Rand, he said he would be home about six thirty. He's not answering his phone. It's not like either of them to disappear like this."

Ryker nodded. "Do you have any reason to suspect someone harmed them?"

"Rand was attacked outside my apartment last night," she said. "Maybe that person—or *persons*—came after him here."

A second vehicle pulled into the lot. Ryker and Chris watched as the black-and-white SUV parked next to Ryker's cruiser. Deputy Jake Gwynn got out. "I heard the call for assistance here at headquarters and came to assist," he said. "I have a key to the building."

"Let's go inside and see what we find," Ryker said. He turned to Chris. "You wait out here."

She wanted to protest but only nodded. While they unlocked the door and went inside, she hugged her arms across her chest and paced beside her car. How could Ryker and Jake be so calm? Sure, she was known to be cool during a search and rescue emergency, but those situations rarely involved anyone she knew. But Rand and Danny were friends, both fit, capable men who wouldn't be pushovers. If something had happened to them, she couldn't help thinking it would be bad.

The deputies emerged from the building and Jake relocked the door. "There's no one in there," Ryker said. "But we found Danny's phone on the floor near the door. He must have dropped it."

"Are you sure Rand didn't have to report back to the hospital?" Jake asked. "Or maybe he's visiting a friend?"

She shook her head. "He wouldn't go back to work without his car. You need to talk to the members of the Vine. Someone told me they're camped out past County Road 14."

"Do you think they had something to do with Rand and Danny?" Jake asked.

"I'm sure they were the ones who attacked Rand and

then me last night," she said. "I can't prove it, but I'm sure of it. Maybe they came back for Rand tonight."

"Why would they do that?" Ryker asked.

"To get back at me?" She shook her head. "I don't know. But please, go talk to them. Rand and Danny might be with them now."

"It wouldn't hurt to go out there," Jake said. "But there's a good chance we're wasting time."

"Do you have a better idea of where to look?" Chris asked.

Ryker pocketed his notebook. "We'll drive out there and take a look," he said. "You go home. We'll be in touch."

"I'm staying at Rand's place," she admitted. "My apartment needs the doors and locks replaced."

"Go there, then," Jake said. "We'll let you know what we find."

They returned to their vehicles and she to hers. The deputies waited for her to drive away, then followed her back toward town. They turned off toward County Road 14 while she continued toward Rand's place. She didn't like the idea of returning to the unfamiliar house alone. At least Harley would be there with her.

And what if Ryker and Jake didn't find Rand and Danny with the Vine? What if someone else had taken them or they had left for some other reason? She might have wasted the deputies' time and put the two men in further danger.

"WE DON'T HAVE proper medical equipment or medications," Rand protested. "We can't help this woman without the right tools."

"We're very good at making do," Jedediah said. "Tell us what you need, and we'll supply a reasonable substitute."

Which was how Rand and Danny found themselves minutes later with a stack of clean towels, a selection of sharp
knives, a sewing kit, a bar of soap, and a bottle of what
looked and smelled like grain alcohol. "I'm not going to
perform surgery without anesthesia," Rand said.

"If you don't operate, she's going to die anyway," Danny
said softly. The two huddled over their patient, having sent
everyone else to wait either outside or against the far wall.
Jedediah had left, but the patient's brother stood nearby,
the gun tucked into the front of his jeans, quickly acces-
sible if he decided he needed to use it again.

The two men knelt beside the woman, and Rand once
more assessed her condition, which he could only classify
as poor. She was barely conscious and mostly unresponsive, her pulse faint. She needed an emergency C-section,
and even then her chances of survival were slim. But he
couldn't do nothing and watch her die. "I can try to turn the
baby," Rand said. "Let's see if we can revive her enough to
help us." He looked up at her brother. "What's her name?"

"Lana," the man said.

"Get down here and talk to her," Rand said.

The brother shook his head and backed away. Exasper-
ated, Rand looked across at the girl, who hadn't spoken and
had scarcely moved since he and Danny entered the truck.
"What's your name?" he asked.

"Serena."

"Serena, is Lana a relative of yours?"

The girl shook her head.

"Then why are you here?" Danny asked.

"It's my job to help the healer."

Rand would have told whoever was in charge that this
was no place for a child so young, but since Serena was

already here, he asked if she would hold Lana's hand and talk to her while he and Danny worked. "She may be able to hear you, even if she doesn't respond," he explained.

Serena nodded. "All right."

Rand looked back at one of the older women against the wall. "I need some ammonia."

"Ammonia?" She looked puzzled.

"The cleaning fluid. You must have some somewhere."

"I'll see what I can find."

Lana's brother moved a little closer, though he didn't kneel beside the pallet. "What's your name?" Danny asked.

"Robert."

"Why did you wait so long to go for help?" Rand asked as he busied himself with cleaning his hands and drying them on one of the towels.

Robert shoved his fingers through his lank hair. "We don't believe in doctors," he said. "We're supposed to trust in the Exalted."

"Are you going to be in trouble for bringing us here?" Danny asked.

Robert shrugged. "Maybe. Probably. Can you help her?"

"We're going to try," Rand said. "But it may be too late."

"Here." The woman returned and thrust a plastic bottle filled with yellow liquid at Rand.

He twisted off the cap and sniffed, his eyes watering. It was ammonia, all right. He poured some on a cloth and held it under Lana's nose. She moaned and turned her head away. "Lana, wake up," he said. "Open your eyes and look at me, please."

Her eyes flickered open, and she stared up at him. Her eyes were dark brown, fringed with long dark lashes. She was probably beautiful when she was feeling better. "My name is Rand," he said. "I'm a doctor, and I'm going to try to help you. I need to try to turn the baby. When I tell you, you need to push."

She nodded. Rand looked at Serena. "Talk to her. Encourage her."

Serena leaned close and whispered to Lana. Rand couldn't hear what she said, and he didn't care. Her job was to try to calm and distract Lana, if that was even possible, given her condition. He nodded to Danny, and the two of them moved down to tackle the dilemma of somehow delivering this baby. Rand was searching for some way to lubricate his hands when the door to the trailer opened, a woman's strident protests breaking the tense silence. "You can't go in there—"

Rand turned to see what the commotion was about just as two Rayford County sheriff's deputies stepped in. "Rand?" one of the deputies asked.

As the officers moved closer, Rand recognized Jake Gwynn. "We need a medical helicopter," he said. "Right away."

"I'll make the call," the other deputy said, and stepped out of the trailer.

Jake took in the woman on the pallet and the people gathered around her. "Are you and Danny okay?" he asked.

"We're fine, but this woman needs emergency surgery."

"No surgery." The older woman who had fetched the ammonia stepped between Rand and Lana. "No hospital. The Exalted forbids it."

"Then if she dies, I'll be happy to testify in the Exalted's murder trial." Rand stood.

Robert stood also. There was no sign of the gun now,

and he moved toward the door. Jake moved to intercept him. "You need to stay here," he said.

The other deputy returned. "This is Ryker Vernon," Jake said. "What happened?"

"Two men grabbed us outside search and rescue headquarters," Danny said. "They forced us to come here to help this woman."

The four men looked down at Lana, who lay still, her breathing slow and labored. "They should have called for help hours ago," Rand said.

"They forced you to come here?" Ryker asked.

"They had a gun," Danny said.

"The Exalted had nothing to do with that," the older woman said. "He forbids the use of violence."

"Apparently, he also forbids outside help, even for a medical emergency," Rand said.

"I think we need to talk to this Exalted person," Jake said. "Where can we find him?"

"I have no idea," Rand said. "I've only spoken to his representative, a man named Jedediah." He turned to Danny. "Let's get Lana ready for transport."

They were making Lana as comfortable as possible when an approaching siren signaled the arrival of the ambulance. Moments later, two paramedics pushed into the trailer, ignoring the orders to stop from some of the onlookers. The first paramedic to enter, a burly fortysomething with close-cropped gray hair, surveyed the room. "We need to get this crowd out of here so we can work."

"You heard the man," Jake said. "Everybody out."

When no one moved, Jake and Ryker began taking hold of people and escorting them out.

Rand introduced himself and Danny and provided

what medical information he had been able to assess, then stepped back to allow the paramedics to take over. By the time he heard the distant throb of a helicopter over the camp, they had started an IV line and fitted Lana with an oxygen mask and various equipment to monitor her vitals. The deputies were still outside, presumably dealing with the other campers. Jedediah didn't make an appearance, and Robert and his fellow kidnapper had disappeared. Serena was gone, too, pulled away by one of the women as the paramedics started their work.

Rand and Danny followed the stretcher out of the trailer and watched as Lana was loaded into the ambulance. She would be driven to the cleared area that had been designated as a landing spot for the helicopter, then rushed to the hospital.

Jake joined Rand and Danny as the ambulance pulled away. "Can you identify the men who kidnapped you?" he asked.

"I can." The crowd of onlookers was mostly moving away now, presumably to the trailers and tents scattered among the trees, their faces indistinguishable in the darkness. "My guess is you won't find them here tonight."

"Give us a description, and we'll conduct a search."

Danny and Rand each described what they knew about the two men who had waylaid them and also provided what they knew about Jedediah.

"How did you know where to find us?" Danny asked when that was done.

"Chris went to SAR headquarters to look for you and found the place locked up tight," Ryker said. "Both your cars were there, and we found your phone on the ground. Carrie called 911 and reported you missing. Chris said she thought the persons who attacked the two of you last night were from the Vine and that they might have gone after you again tonight."

"These men didn't hurt us," Rand said.

"One of them was the woman's brother," Danny said. "I don't think he would have harmed us. I think he was desperate to help his sister."

"Threatening someone with a gun and forcing them to go somewhere against their will is still a crime," Ryker said.

"Let's get you out of here," Jake said.

Rand and Danny shared the back seat of Jake's SUV for the ride to search and rescue headquarters. Neither spoke. Rand was exhausted. The sight of Lana, struggling to stay alive while he was helpless to do anything, would remain with him for a long time. If the Exalted and his followers were willing to sacrifice one of their own for the sake of their misguided beliefs, he could believe they wouldn't hesitate to break laws in order to obey their leader's command to bring a former member back into the fold.

Chapter Ten

Fifteen years ago

Chris, drowsing under the covers in her bunk bed in her family's trailer at the Vine's camp, woke to raised voices. She pulled back the curtain over the bunk and peered toward the glow of light from the other end of the small trailer. Her father sounded angry about something.

"I'm going to talk to him. This isn't right."

"He's made up his mind," her mother said. "You'll never get anywhere arguing with him."

"There must be some misunderstanding. Jedediah got the message wrong. The Exalted has children—daughters. Would he want one of them married off when she's only twelve? Not to mention he already has a wife his age. It's just sick."

"Lower your voice." Mom sounded afraid. "You don't want to let anyone hear you say that."

"It's not right, you know that."

"I know. But what are we going to do? He owns this trailer. He owns everything we have."

"You don't have to remind me," her father said. "I was the one foolish enough to turn everything over to him."

"You weren't foolish. You believed in the message. We're

supposed to share with each other. No one has more than anyone else."

"I still believe that. But not if it means giving him my daughter. I'll talk to him. I'm sure I can make him understand."

"What if he won't listen to you?" her mother asked.

"He will. He has to."

More conversation, but too soft for Chris to hear. A few moments later, the door to the trailer opened and closed. Chris waited but heard nothing more. Finally, she slipped out of bed and padded on bare feet to the front of the trailer. Her mother sat on the edge of the sofa, head in her hands. Was she crying?

Chris hurried to her. "What's wrong?" she asked. "Where is Daddy?" She didn't call him *Daddy* much anymore. It sounded too babyish. But she was too scared to worry about that now.

Her mother pulled her close, arms squeezing her tight. "It's okay," she said, and wiped her eyes with her fingers.

"Where did Daddy go?" Chris asked.

Her mother sniffed. "He went to talk to the Exalted."

"About me?"

Her mother hesitated, then nodded. "Yes." She pulled Chris into her lap even though Chris was too big for that; her feet almost touched the floor when she sat on her mother's lap.

"Helen says there's going to be a wedding soon," Chris said. "That I'll be a bride and wear a white dress and have a big party just for me."

Her mother studied her, deep lines across her forehead. "Do you know what it means to be a bride?" she asked.

Chris thought for a moment. "Helen says I have to live

with the Exalted and do what he tells me." Then she said something she had never dared say before: "I don't want to live with him."

Her mother hugged her tightly again. "Maybe your father can talk him into waiting until you're a little older," she said.

Chris didn't think that when she was older she would want to marry the Exalted, either, but she didn't say anything. "You should go back to bed," her mother said. "It's not even six o'clock yet."

"I'm awake," Chris said. "And hungry. Can I have breakfast?"

Her mother made breakfast; then they both dressed and Chris helped her mother clean house, which didn't take long because the trailer was small and they didn't have much stuff. Mom tried to be extra cheerful, but she kept glancing out the window. "Shouldn't Dad be back by now?" Chris asked after a couple of hours.

"The Exalted probably sent him to do some work," Mom said. Everyone in the Vine was expected to pitch in. For the men, that often meant building things, cutting trees, or digging ditches, latrines or garden beds.

Chris did her lessons. Children in the Vine didn't go to school. Instead, the parents taught them. Some children didn't have to learn anything at all, but Chris's parents made her read and study math, reading, geography, history and science every day. She didn't mind so much. Most of the time the lessons were interesting, and she usually found them easy.

Her mother got out a quilt she was working on, but often, when Chris looked up from her schoolwork, she found her mother staring out the front window, her hands idle.

They ate lunch without Dad. By three o'clock, her mother could hardly sit still. She put away her quilting. "I'm going to look for your father," she said. "Lock the door behind me, and don't let anyone in unless it's me or your dad. Do you understand?"

Chris nodded. "What am I supposed to tell anyone who comes by?"

"Don't tell them anything," Mom said. "Stay quiet and let them think no one is home."

Chris wanted to ask what her mother was afraid of, but she didn't. Instead, she turned the lock after her mother was gone and sat on the sofa to wait.

She was back in half an hour. "Jedediah told me your father left the Exalted's home this morning with some other men. They went into the woods to pick mushrooms."

"Isn't it the wrong time of year for mushrooms?" Chris asked. Always before, they had looked for mushrooms in the spring and fall, when they would pop up after wet weather. Now it was midsummer, warm and dry.

"Maybe this was a different kind of mushroom," her mother said. "Or someone found some by a spring or something. Come, help me peel potatoes. We'll make a special dinner. Maybe we'll even make a cake."

Making the cake, and the potatoes and vegetables and meat loaf, took a while, but six o'clock—the hour they usually ate supper—passed with no sign of her father. Her mother filled a plate and told Chris to sit down at the table and eat it, but Chris only stared at the food, her stomach too queasy for her to even think of putting anything into her mouth.

A little before nine o'clock, they heard voices outside. Mom rushed to the door, then, with a cry, opened it to admit

Jedediah and a man Chris didn't know. Between them, they carried her father, his face gray, his hair and clothes wet. "He ate some of the mushrooms he found," Jedediah said. "I think they must have been poisonous."

They carried her father past Chris to her parents' bed at the back of the trailer. Mom hurried after them. Chris tried to follow, but Jedediah shut the door in her face.

A few minutes later, the door opened again and the two men emerged. "What's going on?" Chris asked.

"We're going to fetch the healing woman," the man she didn't know said. Jedediah only scowled at her.

When they were gone, Chris went to the bedroom door and knocked. "Mom?" she called.

"You can't come in," her mother called. "Go to your room and wait for me."

Chris didn't really have a room, just a bunk bed with a curtain to separate it from the rest of the trailer. Not knowing what else to do, she went there and sat. She switched on the light her father had fixed up for her and took her sketchbook from the lidded box at the end of the bed that he had made for her art supplies. She turned to a fresh page and began to draw. When she started, she had no idea what she would sketch, but after a few moments, the figure of a man took shape. The Exalted, but not the beautiful, caring figure people often praised. This was the Exalted with his mouth twisted in a sneer, his eyes glaring, deep lines marring his forehead and running alongside his mouth. Instead of an angel, this man was a demon.

After a while, Chris began to get sleepy. She drifted off and woke up much later to an old woman shaking her— Elizabeth, one of the healers. "Come and say goodbye to your father," she said.

"Where is he going?" Chris asked. She glanced over at the sketchbook and was relieved to see she had remembered to close it before she fell asleep.

"He is going to his reward," Elizabeth said. "He ate poison, and there is nothing I can do for him."

Chris began to cry, then to wail. Elizabeth shook her. "Quiet!" she ordered. "He's going to a better place. There's no reason for you to be sad."

Even at twelve, Chris knew that was one of the most ridiculous things anyone had ever said. He was her father. He belonged here with her. There was no better place.

But she fell silent and allowed Elizabeth to lead her into her parents' bedroom. Her mother held out her hand. Chris took it, and her mother pulled her close. She stared at her father, who lay with his eyes closed, his skin that awful gray, his face all hollows. He didn't even look like himself. "Give him a kiss," Elizabeth commanded.

Chris shook her head and buried her face in her mother's shoulder. "It's all right," her mother murmured. "You're safe here with me."

No one said anything else. Chris heard movement, and when she looked up again, she and her mother were alone with her father. "Where did they all go?" Chris whispered.

Her mother had to try a couple of times before she could speak. "They went to prepare for…for the funeral," she said.

Chris looked at her father. He didn't look any different to her. "Is he…dead?" she asked.

"Yes," her mother said. "He's gone." Then she started to cry. Chris cried, too, grateful there was no one to tell them it was wrong to do so.

Everything about the next few days was a blur. They buried her father in the woods the next morning, his body wrapped in a bedsheet and lowered into a deep hole, far away from camp. Everyone came and gathered around the little grave, and when they were all assembled, the Exalted arrived. The crowd parted to allow him to draw close. He was dressed all in white, his hair and face shining. He smiled as if this was a happy occasion, and he talked about what a good man her father was and how he had moved on to a better place than this.

When he finished speaking, men with shovels moved forward and began to fill in the grave. The scent of fresh earth filled Chris's nose, and she began to sob again.

A hand rested on her shoulder, heavy and warm. She looked up and stared into the Exalted's eyes. "Your father is gone," he said. "I will be your father now. I will be your brother and uncle. And your husband. Soon." He smiled, but Chris could only shiver.

Chris knew then that she didn't like the Exalted, no matter how wonderful people said he was. But she kept that knowledge to herself. She was pretty sure if she said something like that out loud, she would be struck by lightning or something worse. If she was the only one who thought someone was bad when everyone said he was good, there must be something wrong with her.

Her mother was much quieter after that. Sad.

Three days later, Helen came to their trailer. "It's time to measure Elita for her wedding dress," she said.

Her mother's face paled. "So soon?"

"Now that your husband is gone, the Exalted believes it's even more important that he take Elita under his wing." Helen pulled out a tape measure. "Fetch a chair for her to stand on."

Her mother brought a chair from the kitchen table.

"Shouldn't there be a period of mourning?" she asked as she helped Chris to stand on the chair.

"Mourning won't bring back the dead." Helen wrapped the tape measure around Chris's chest, over the gentle swelling her mother had told her would one day be breasts. "Better to focus on the joy of this occasion."

Neither Chris nor her mother said anything after Helen left. What was there to say? No one disobeyed the Exalted. It would be like disobeying God. The next day, her mother worked at the farmers market stand the Vine operated at the fairgrounds. She came home later than usual. "Something terrible has happened," she said. "Someone stole the money from our booth. The cash box was there one moment, and then it was gone."

"Was there a lot of money in it?" Chris asked.

"Several hundred dollars. Jedediah is very upset." Jedediah was the treasurer for the Vine, in charge of all the money the group earned from selling crafts, produce, firewood and anything else. All the money went to Jedediah, who doled it out as needed.

Not long after Chris's mother had set supper on the table, someone pounded on the door, hard enough to make the trailer shake. Mom opened it, and Jedediah and a trio of men filled the small front room. "We need to search this place," Jedediah said.

"What for?" Mom asked.

"We're looking for the money that was stolen. We're searching the homes of everyone who worked that booth today."

Was he accusing her mother of being a thief? Chris expected her mother to be upset about this. Instead, she stepped back and bowed her head. "Of course," she said. "I have nothing to hide."

For the next hour, the four men searched every inch of the trailer. They emptied all the clothing from the dresser and dumped all Chris's art supplies on the bed. She thought of the picture of the Exalted—the devil picture—in her sketchbook. When they found it, would they punish her? But they only flipped through the book, paying no attention to the drawings. They took the food from the refrigerator and opened every jar and bottle as if they expected to find coins and bills instead of mayonnaise and ketchup.

All they found was five dollars and forty-two cents in change in an old pickle jar. Members of the Vine were allowed to keep this change when they sold cans they picked up on the side of the highway, so Jedediah reluctantly set the jar back on the dresser. "There's nothing here," he said at last, and the men left.

Mom sank into a chair. She looked very pale, but when she saw Chris watching her, she forced a smile. "That was upsetting, but it's over now," she said. "There's nothing for you to worry about. Why don't you get ready for bed?"

Chris started to point out that it was an hour before her bedtime but thought better of it. She washed her face and hands, then put on her pajamas and crawled under the covers. Her mother kissed her forehead and pulled the curtain over the bunk. Within minutes, Chris was asleep.

It was still dark when she woke again. Her mother sat on the edge of the bunk. "Get dressed," Mom said. "We're going to leave now." She handed Chris a pair of jeans and a T-shirt. "I packed a bag for us. I put in as many of your art supplies as I could, but we can't take everything."

"Where are we going?" Chris asked, pulling off her pajamas and sliding into the jeans.

"We're leaving the Vine," her mother said. "And we're never coming back."

Chapter Eleven

If Chris was upset about what had happened to Rand and Danny, she kept her feelings hidden. She was clearly relieved Rand was all right, but when he thanked her for alerting the sheriff's deputies to what must have happened to them, she dismissed his thanks. "It was a lucky guess," she said. "I'm glad it worked out."

"Why were they so set against calling in medical help for that woman?" he asked. "Is it because they don't believe in medicine? Or they think it's some kind of spiritual weakness to rely on doctors?"

"It's mostly because they don't want outsiders coming into the camp," she said. "We were always told we didn't need anyone but each other and the Exalted."

"Because outsiders might see something illegal they shouldn't see?" Rand asked.

She blew out a breath. "I don't know. I was taught—all the kids were—that outsiders were dangerous. That they would take us away from our families and sell us to people who would do bad things to us. For the first few months after Mom and I left the Vine, I was terrified to let her out of my sight or to talk to anyone."

"The woman I tried to help, Lana, looked younger than

you—maybe not even out of her teens. I wonder if you knew her."

"I've been away for a long time," she said. "I doubt I know any of the current members. I don't remember anyone called Lana."

"Jedediah is still there," Rand said. "There are probably others you knew who are still with the group."

"Maybe I would know their names," she said. "But I don't know them. I never did."

Her tone was defiant, her expression fierce. When she turned away, he didn't press her. He knew plenty of soldiers who refused to discuss things that had happened during their military service. Maybe it was the same for survivors of cults.

Three days after Rand returned home, Sheriff Travis Walker and Deputy Ryker Vernon came to Rand's house at four thirty, shortly after he arrived home after a shift at the hospital. "We wanted to bring you up to date on a few things," Travis said after Rand had welcomed the lawmen inside.

Chris came in from the kitchen and stopped short. "Oh, hello." She glanced at Rand. "Is something wrong?"

"We just have some updates," Travis said. "For both of you. Sit down, please."

They sat—Rand on the sofa and Chris in a chair facing him. "First of all, I'm sorry to tell you that Lana and her baby died," Travis said.

"Yes, I know," Rand said. "I had a colleague track her down for me."

Chris turned to him. "You didn't tell me."

"I didn't want to upset you," he said.

Chris studied her hands, knotted in her lap. "It's just such a sad story."

"We searched the camp for her brother and the other man you described," Ryker said. "We were told they had been banished."

"Did you look for any fresh graves in the woods?" Chris asked.

Rand felt the shock of her words. "You think they were murdered?" he asked.

She looked as if she regretted saying anything.

"Why graves?" Travis prompted.

She shifted in her chair. "I don't have any proof, but other people who did things the Exalted didn't like had a way of disappearing or meeting with accidents or sudden illness."

"Your father," Travis said.

"Yes. And there were others. Anyone who complained too much or spread what the Exalted deemed to be 'radical ideas,' and certainly anyone who opposed the Exalted, was soon gone, and everyone else was forbidden to even say their names."

"We'll continue searching for the two men," Travis said.

"What about this guy who calls himself the Exalted, Edmund Harrison?" Rand asked. "His refusal to allow anyone to summon outside help is the reason Lana died."

Travis's expression tightened. "Harrison denies having that policy, and no one would admit otherwise when we spoke with them," he said. "We researched his history, and he has no criminal record."

"The official story is that Lana herself refused help and that her brother went to fetch help against her wishes," Ryker said.

"The Exalted has brainwashed everyone to see outsiders as the enemy," Chris said. "If you bring anyone from outside into the group, you risk having families torn apart, horrible diseases inflicted on the group by way of things like vaccinations and medications, children forced to attend public schools, et cetera. If there's a bogeyman the Exalted and his enforcers can conjure to keep people obedient, he's happy to preach about it until fear is as much a part of them as breathing."

"He says they have no record of you ever being a member of his group, and he doesn't understand why you would be so fixated on them," Travis said.

Color flooded her face. "I'm not lying. My parents were members of the Vine, and we lived with them for seven years. And you were there the day Jedediah came up to me and said it was time for me to marry the Exalted."

"Edmund Harrison says you misunderstood," Travis said.

The lines around her mouth tightened. "There was no misunderstanding."

"Has he made any more threats against you?" Travis asked.

"He doesn't know where I am right now," she said. "But once he does, he'll send someone after me."

"Why is he so focused on you?" Ryker asked.

"No one defies him," she said. "My mother and I did. He's like a spoiled child that way. Deny him something and he's going to do everything he can to get it." She smoothed her hand down the tattoos on her left arm. "But he doesn't want me, really. He just wants to punish me. Maybe make an example of me."

"We interviewed him," Travis said. "By Zoom. He is supposedly in Texas right now—on business, he said. He denies knowing you. Denies having more than one wife. Denies keeping anyone in the group against their will."

"I'm sure he told you the group is all about peace, love and free will," she said.

"That's about it," Ryker agreed.

"Harrison told us the group planned to leave Colorado and move on to Oklahoma," Travis said. "When we returned to the camp yesterday, everyone was gone. They didn't leave one piece of trash or so much as a food scrap behind."

"Where did they go?" Rand asked.

"We don't know," Travis said. "They may have decided they were getting too much attention from law enforcement."

"They're probably putting as much distance between us and them as possible," Ryker added.

Chris said nothing, though Rand felt the tension radiating off her. "Is there anything else you think we need to know?" Travis asked.

"Don't believe it when they tell you they're just a close-knit community of nature lovers," Chris said. "And I don't think they've left the area."

"We'll keep our eyes and ears open," Travis said. "Let us know if you hear anything."

Ryker and Travis left. Chris stared out the front window after them, then began to pace. "The sheriff doesn't believe me," she said. "He thinks I'm making up a story to get attention or something."

"He didn't say that," Rand said. "I think he's trying to look at the case from every angle." He moved in beside her and put his hand on her shoulder. "I believe you."

She wouldn't look at him. She held herself rigid, jaw tight, as if fighting for control. "I feel like I'm waiting for something to happen," she said after a long silence. "Something bad."

"You believe they're still here," Rand said.

"They've been pursuing me for fifteen years," she said. "Why leave when they've gotten this close?"

He nodded. While some might dismiss Chris's protests, his experience with the ruthlessness of his sister's cult made him inclined to believe her. He wanted to put his arm around her and try to comfort her, but he wasn't sure she would be receptive. "What can I do?" he asked instead.

She pressed her lips together, arms crossed, shoulders hunched. Then she raised her eyes to his. "Tell me about your sister," she said.

CHRIS SAT ON the sofa and patted the cushion next to her. She needed a distraction to pull her out of the worry cycle she was in. "I want to hear about her, if you don't mind talking about it," she said.

Rand sat, the cushion compressing under his weight, shifting her toward him. He leaned forward, hands clasped, elbows on knees. "I haven't talked about Teri in a long time," he said. "But I'd like to tell you."

Chris let out a breath, some of the tension easing. She had been afraid he would shut her down—as she herself might have done in his shoes. "She was younger than you?"

"Yes. Nineteen. I was completing my first tour in Afghanistan when she met this group of people. At a local coffee shop, she said. They approached her table and asked if they could sit down. The place was crowded, so she said yes. They fell into conversation and apparently talked for hours. They introduced themselves as volunteers, working on a project to help the poor in the area. Teri always had a soft heart and wanted to help people. They picked up on that right away and used her sympathy to reel her in."

"The Vine taught the same technique," Chris said. "Identify what you have in common with the person, what they are concerned about or appear to need, and play up that connection."

"There was a guy in the group—Mark or Mike or Mitch, I never did learn his real name. In the group, he was known as Starfire. They all had names like that—Rainbow and Cloud, Surfer and Starfire. The next thing I heard, Teri was calling herself Aurora. She quit school and moved out of the dorm and into a camper van with Starfire, and then the group left town. My parents were frantic when they contacted me, hoping I had heard from her. But I hadn't heard a thing."

"What did you do?"

"There was nothing I could do. I was in a field hospital in a war zone. I couldn't leave. My parents contacted the police but were told if Teri left of her own free will, there wasn't anything they could do. Mom and Dad had a couple of phone calls from her saying she was fine and they didn't need to worry, and that was it."

"We had people join the Vine who left families behind," Chris said. "I never thought much about the anguish those parents must have felt. And their brothers and sisters."

"One day Teri was with us, then she was gone, with a group of people we didn't know anything about. On one hand, I understood what the police were telling us. An adult has the right to make her own decisions. But putting together what I learned when I researched online and what I heard from my parents, the group felt wrong to me."

"What did you find out online?" she asked.

"Mostly there were postings on various websites from relatives who were desperate to get in touch with their missing children or siblings. A few complaints from businesses in areas where the group had stayed, alleging that members had stolen items or harassed customers."

"What was the name of the group?"

"They called themselves Atlantis or the Seekers."

Chris shook her head. "I haven't heard of them, but most people have never heard of the Vine either. These groups try to keep a low profile."

"I was able to piece together some of their story after I was discharged from the army. By then, she had been with the group for almost two years. They made a living by recruiting members, who were obligated to turn over all their money to the group. They also begged and, I think, stole, though they always left town before anyone reported them to the local law enforcement."

Chris nodded. "The Vine did that, too—made new members turn over all their assets. They were told they were contributing to the group, but I think most of the money went to the Exalted. While we lived in tents and trailers, he had a fancy motorhome and, supposedly, owned houses in several states. He traveled a lot, managing his various properties, and often delivered his messages to us via videotaped lectures. The rare times he did come to our camp were big occasions. Everyone turned out for a glimpse of him."

"From the research I did, a lot of these groups operate the same way," Rand said.

"What happened to your sister?" Chris asked. He had said she'd committed suicide, but how? When?

"It took me a long time to find her," he said. "By the time I located her, she had been with the group over two years and was fully brainwashed, and refused my pleas to leave the group."

"You spoke to her?"

"Yes. I tracked the group down to a little town in Eastern Oregon. Teri was there. She looked terrible. She had lost weight and wore this shapeless sack of a dress, her hair uncombed in these kind of dreadlocks. She had lost a front tooth—she wouldn't say how. And when I tried to talk to her, she said she wasn't allowed to talk to outsiders and ran away."

"Oh, Rand." Chris laid a hand on his arm.

"I went after her. I told her I was her brother and she owed me more than she owed her so-called friends. I was furious. I told her all those people had done was take her away from her home and family, take her money, and give her nothing in return. She told me I didn't understand, that the inner peace the Seekers had given her was worth all the money in the world. She said they were her family now and she didn't need anyone else. Then she left."

Chris felt sick. "All of that sounds familiar," she said. "It's the kind of thing we were all drilled on saying. I never saw it, but my mother said a couple of times families had tracked down their loved ones to one of our camps. The Exalted had people who were trained in how to deal with them to get them to leave."

"What did they say?"

"What your sister said—that we were that person's family now and they didn't need anyone else."

"I wanted to grab Teri and drag her out of there, but I figured that would only get me arrested for kidnapping. One of the Seekers said if I laid a hand on Aurora that he would call the police. So I let her be. But I kept track of the group as best I could."

"Not easy to do," Chris said. "The Vine was expert at packing up in the middle of the night and showing up across the country a week later. Mom was able to find a few people who have family who are members. They sometimes let her know where the group is living at the moment, but even they can't always keep up."

"I had a buddy from the military who was a private detective, and he took an interest in the group and did what he could to track them," Rand said. "He kept me up to date. About six months later I had a meeting in California, not far from the latest Seeker gathering. They weren't camping this time but were renting, or maybe squatting, in an old hotel. The place was a dump, with a leaking roof, water damage to the walls and no electricity. I couldn't see that they had done any work on it, except to erect a large brightly painted sign announcing that it was the Atlantis Center for Enlightenment."

He fell silent. Chris waited, and found herself matching her breathing to his own. When the silence stretched to minutes, she asked, "Your sister was there?"

"She was. I played it cool this time. I gave a fake name at the door and said I was interested in learning about Atlantis. I was taken to a room, and three disciples entered. They were dressed in jeans and T-shirts and looked very normal. They asked me a lot of questions about how I had found out about them, what I was seeking, et cetera. I gave vague answers, and they seemed pretty suspicious at first, but after I said I had inherited a lot of money from my grandfather and was looking for a worthy group that would benefit from the cash, their demeanor changed. They invited me to have dinner with them that evening.

"Teri was there. She was one of the women who were serving the food. I guess they probably cooked it too. She didn't look any better than the last time I had seen her, and when she saw me, she dropped a platter of vegetables and ran from the room. I almost turned over a chair going after her. I cornered her in an upstairs bedroom and begged her to leave with me. She just cried and shook her head and said she couldn't.

"I told her I wasn't leaving without her. One of the men threatened to call the police, and I told him to do it—that I had plenty of proof there were people there being held against their will. That was a bluff, but it worked. They backed off."

Chris could see it all in her mind, from his frightened sister to the threatening Seekers—and Rand caught in the middle but determined to win. "What happened?" she asked.

"I took Teri by the hand and led her out of there. She came with me, still crying. I drove four hours away, checked us into a hotel under a fake name, paid cash for the room and ordered pizza. She started crying again when she saw the pizza. She said she hadn't had any since she had left with the group. I asked her what she had been eating, and she said they had a special diet of only natural foods and they had to fast three days a week. She said that was healthier, and it took everything in me not to point out that she didn't look healthy.

"After we ate, she fell asleep. She looked exhausted, and I know I was."

Ominous silence followed. Silence with weight. Chris

had trouble breathing. For a long time Rand didn't say anything, his jaw tight, hands clenched.

"When I woke the next morning, she was gone," he said finally. "She had run away in the middle of the night. I went back to the abandoned hotel looking for her, but everyone there said they hadn't seen her. The police couldn't help me. I lost it at them, and they ended up threatening to arrest me. I stayed in town for a while, watching the group, but I never saw Teri again."

"But you believe she had returned to the group?" Chris asked.

"I know she did. Three months later, my parents received a phone call from someone with the group, telling them Teri's body was at the morgue in Bend, Oregon, and they could claim her body if they wanted. They said Teri had killed herself. The coroner said she had slit her wrists. She left a note—a lot of incoherent nonsense about destiny and enlightenment and final bliss."

Tears stung her eyes—tears for him and for his poor, hurting sister. "It wasn't your fault," she said.

"I could have handled it better. I could have forced her to come with me and taken her to a deprogrammer or something."

"That could have failed too." She rubbed his arm. "It wasn't your fault."

He let out a shaky breath. "The police in Bend investigated, but they couldn't find anything suspicious. The group left town and dropped off the radar. The last I heard, they were in South America."

"I'm so sorry about your sister," she said. The words seemed so paltry compared to what he had suffered, but she had nothing else to give.

"I haven't talked about this with anyone for a long time." He looked at her, his eyes damp but his expression calm. "You're a good listener."

She leaned closer, drawn to him, pulled in by the sadness in his eyes and a sense of shared grief. She hadn't lost a sister but a father, and the chance to grow up without the fear that had dogged her all her life. Her gaze shifted to his lips. She recalled the connection they had shared before, and she wanted that again.

She meant to kiss him gently, but the strength of her longing drove her harder than she had intended. He gripped her shoulders and responded with a gentling pressure of his own. He wanted this, too, his body seemed to say, but he wanted to savor the moment, to linger over the sensation of the two of them together.

She leaned into him, letting him take her weight, his arm wrapped around her. She could definitely get used to this...

She opened her eyes to find him looking at her as if he could see everything. The idea was unnerving, and she pulled away. "Something wrong?" he asked.

"No. Of course not." She sat up straighter, putting a little distance between them. "I really like you. A lot. But I'm not ready to take things any further."

"I respect that," he said. "No pressure. I want you to feel safe here."

"I can't feel safe anywhere as long as I know the Vine is so close by." She laid her head on his shoulder. "But being here is better than being alone."

"It is." He squeezed her shoulder. "Better for me too."

Chapter Twelve

The next morning Rand awoke early—a habit from so many dawn hospital shifts. He dressed and moved to the kitchen, hearing no indication Chris was awake. Good. She had looked exhausted when she had retired to her room last night. He had felt drained, too, but not in a bad way. Revisiting the events surrounding Teri's death had been wrenching, but cleansing too.

He had coffee brewing and was chopping vegetables for omelets when Chris came into the kitchen. "I thought you would have left for work," she said as she headed for the coffeepot.

"I have a couple of days off." He began cracking eggs into a bowl. "Do you want to do something today to get out of the house? Maybe a hike or a drive in the mountains?"

She sipped the coffee and closed her eyes, a look of satisfaction tugging up the corners of her mouth. He almost chuckled. He had experienced those first-sip nirvana moments himself. Then the smile faded, and she opened her eyes again. "I should probably check in with Jasmine and see if my doors have been repaired. Now that the Vine has moved on, I should go home."

"Do you really think they've moved away?" Rand asked. He began sautéing the peppers, onions and mushrooms.

"Maybe they've just relocated to a new campsite the sheriff doesn't know about."

She cradled her mug in both hands. "Honestly, I would be surprised if they gave up on me so easily," she said. "They've been pursuing me for years. This is the first time they've gotten close enough to confront me face-to-face. That must feel like a victory to them."

"I agree," he said. "Groups like this count on people underestimating them." The way he had underestimated the Seekers. "I think they're probably lying low and waiting for another opportunity."

She nodded.

"I think you should stay here until we're sure there's not a threat." He turned back to the stove and added the eggs to the pan. "So, what about taking a drive into the mountains today? Maybe find a trail to hike?"

"Sure. That's a great idea." She straightened. "Is there anything I can do to help with breakfast?"

"Get two plates out of that cabinet there, will you?" He added cheese to the omelet, then folded it over.

She brought out the plates, and he divided the omelet between them; then they carried the meal to the table. "You've lived here longer than I have," he said. "Where would be a good place for us to check out this morning?"

They discussed options. Chris's mood seemed to lift as they talked. Rand hoped the prospect of a day spent with him—not just the momentary distraction from her concerns about the Vine—was at least partially responsible for her change in mood.

THEY WERE CLEARING the dishes when Chris's phone rang. She didn't recognize the number. "Hello?" she asked, expecting a junk call.

"I'm panicking and I need someone to talk me down off a ledge." Bethany sounded breathless.

Chris laughed. "What's going on?" She moved into the living room.

"I'm serious. Something terrible has happened. I need help."

"What's wrong?" Chris gripped the phone more tightly. "What can I do?"

"I'm thinking we could blow up the stretch of highway leading into Eagle Mountain, but my family probably wouldn't let an obstacle like that stop them. Plus, there's the jail time to think of, not to mention I'm afraid of explosives."

"What are you talking about? You're not making sense."

"Sorry. But I'm so freaked out. My family has decided if I won't come back to Vermont to them, they will come here."

"Your family is coming to visit you? That doesn't sound so bad." Leave it to Bethany—who clearly liked drama—to make something like this into a big deal.

"No, they're moving here. All of them. My mom and dad and all three of my brothers."

"Oh, wow. What brought this on?"

"They're not just moving here—they're buying the Jeep-rental business I work for. And not just the business but the building it's in. Where my apartment is located. So now they're going to be my bosses and my landlords as well as my parents."

"Yikes. You weren't kidding when you said they're overprotective."

"I knew the business was for sale, but I never imagined my parents would buy it. Mom and Dad said they're ready to try something new, and they're super excited we're all going to be together again."

"And your brothers are coming too. How old are they?"

"Aaron is twenty-seven. The twins, Carter and Dalton, are twenty-four. The twins are going to work for Mom and Dad. Which means they'll be my coworkers." She groaned. "The oldest, Aaron, has a job in town, too, though he wouldn't tell me what it was. Which is just like him. He's the devious one among us."

"I'm sorry," Chris said. "But obviously, they love you very much."

Bethany sighed. "They do. And I love them. But they still treat me like a child. And my brothers—it's like being surrounded by a bunch of spies. Once, when I was fourteen, some girlfriends and I toilet-papered another girl's house, and I wasn't back home before Mom and Dad knew about it. They made me get out of bed at six in the morning to clean up the mess I made. And forget dating. Until I was eighteen, I had to double-date with one of my brothers and his girlfriend. Even after that, bringing someone home to meet the family was a huge ordeal. I can't tell you how many guys I never heard from again after they got the third degree from the Ames men."

Chris laughed. "I know it's not funny to you, but it's so different from how I grew up. It was just my mom and me. I used to think it would be great to be part of a big, loving family." A real family. Not one like the Vine.

"You're right. Most of the time it is fun. I do love them, and I know they love me. But this is too much."

"Maybe you can find another apartment. That might help some."

"Maybe. But this apartment is one of the perks of the

job. It's part of my compensation package. I could look for a new job, but I really like this. It's a perfect fit for me. What am I going to do?"

"I'm not sure I'm the right person to give advice to anyone," Chris said.

"Of course you are. You have your own apartment. You're an artist. A full-time artist. That's an incredible accomplishment. And I hear you've been seeing a certain very good-looking doctor."

Chris made a face, even though Bethany couldn't see her. "Where did you hear that?"

"Oh, you know. Someone saw you two together and told someone else, and the next thing you know, the two of you are practically engaged. You're not, are you? Engaged, I mean?"

"No." Chris's stomach quivered at the thought. "Rand and I are just friends."

"Okay, so you have a hot friend. Anyway, I bet you never did anything in your life you didn't want to do, no matter what your friends and family said. So tell me what to do about this."

"I don't think there's a lot you can do. If they've bought this business and are determined to move to Eagle Mountain, you can't stop them. Maybe practice smiling and thanking them for whatever advice they feel compelled to hand out—then do whatever you want without feeling guilty. Maybe that will help them to see you in a new light."

"You make it sound easy, but you haven't met my family. They can be very persuasive."

Now Chris felt queasy as she recalled some of the methods of "persuasion" the Vine had used. "They're not, well, abusive, are they?"

"What? No! Of course not!"

"I'm sorry. I had to make sure."

"I forget you haven't met them yet. You know the phrase 'killing them with kindness'? My parents are masters of that technique. I don't think it's possible to really love someone to death, but if it were, my parents could do it. And my brothers are all so good looking and charming they have every female, and half the men, in our hometown conned into believing they're perfect angels. It's infuriating, really."

"I can't wait to meet these people," Chris said, suppressing a laugh.

"Oh, you'll meet them. They'll know everyone in town inside of two weeks. They're that kind of friendly. And they'll ask you all kinds of nosy questions. Feel free to ignore them, but I probably don't have to tell you that. Please teach me how to fight my natural tendency to want people to like me. It's painful and embarrassing, I tell you."

"No, it's sweet." Chris was laughing now; she couldn't help it. But not at Bethany. The young woman was really starting to grow on her.

"No, you're sweet to say so." She sighed. "Anyway, I feel better having gotten all that off my chest. What are you up to today?"

"I'm going hiking."

"By yourself? Be careful. I don't want to get a call later that we have to go rescue you. Not to mention—how embarrassing would that be?"

"No, I'm going with…" She started to say *a friend* but decided to share a little bit more with Bethany. "With Rand."

"Oooh. Have fun. Not that you wouldn't. He really has that hot-older-guy thing going on. I want to hear all about it later. Or not. I'm nosy, but feel free to tell me to mind my own. One good thing about having three overbearing brothers is that I have a very thick skin."

Chris laughed again. "Have a good day, Bethany. And I'm sure things will work out with your parents."

"If it doesn't, I'll be living with them when I'm forty, after they've scared away every single man within a hundred-mile radius. But it won't be so terrible. My mom's a great cook, and my dad never beats me at cards."

Chris ended the call and returned to the kitchen, where Rand was finishing the dishes. "How old are you?" she asked.

"I'm forty-one. Why?"

"No reason. You just seem…younger." She knew he was a little older than she was, but fourteen years older? Then again, there were plenty of times when she felt decades older than someone like Bethany, who was probably much closer to Chris's age than Rand.

"Having second thoughts about hanging out with an old man?" he asked.

"No. I appreciate maturity."

"Ouch!"

She turned away, smiling to herself. Bethany was right. Rand was definitely a hot older guy. There were worse ways to spend a summer afternoon than with him.

RAND DROVE HIS SUV as far as he could into the high country above town, until they reached the roads only a Jeep or similar vehicle could navigate. They chose a trail that promised a hike to a high mountain lake and set out, Harley trotting ahead. The trail climbed gradually, and they passed areas where wildflowers grew hip-deep in an extravagance of pink, purple, yellow and white. Bees and hummingbird moths wove erratic paths between blossoms, heavy with pollen, and the air was as perfumed as a boudoir. Harley stalked through the grass, then burst out ahead of them, shaking a shower of flower petals from his coat and grinning in that way dogs have, an expression of ecstasy.

"Have you been married before?" Chris asked when they had been hiking a while.

"Where did that question come from?"

She shrugged. "If you're forty-one, I figured there was a chance you'd been married before."

"I haven't."

"Why not?"

His first instinct was to say *because I haven't*, but Chris deserved something less flippant. "Let's see—six years of medical school and residency, terrible hours and no money, three years in a surgical unit in a war zone... Not conducive to long-term relationships."

"That only takes you up to, what, thirty?"

"Three more years in a military hospital stateside. I had girlfriends but nothing ever lasted." He shrugged. "Marriage is a big decision. One I don't want to make unless I'm sure."

"Fair enough."

"Does it bother you that I'm so much older than you?"

"I didn't even think about it until Bethany said something."

"What did Bethany say?"

Chris smiled. "I'm not going to tell you. It will go to your head. But she referred to you as an older guy."

"I like to think I've got a lot of good years left. For what it's worth, when we first met, I thought you were older. Not because of your looks but because of your attitude."

"Guess I'm just an old soul. And today I'm just enjoying

being in a beautiful place." She sent him a look that held a little sizzle. "With you."

All right, then. He suddenly felt a foot taller—but also like it was time to dial back the tension. "Race you to the top of the next ridge."

Rand beat her to the top, but just barely. They stood side by side, looking out across the mountain peaks and rolling valleys. "What is that down there?" She indicated a cluster of colored shapes in the shadow of a jagged pinnacle.

Rand dug his binoculars from his pack and focused on the spot. As he adjusted the focus, a dozen or more colorful tents came into view. "It's a bunch of tents and people," he said. "Didn't Danny announce something about a scout group up here?"

"That's next month." She held out her hand. "Let me see."

She studied the encampment for a long moment, her body tense. Then she returned the binoculars to him. When she didn't say anything, he asked, "Do you think it's the Vine?"

She nodded. "I can't prove it. And I'm afraid if I report this to the sheriff, he'll think I'm either paranoid or vying for more attention."

He scanned the area again. He counted at least fifteen smaller tents and several large ones. Lots of people—men, women and children—milled about. "It could be them," he said. He lowered the binoculars again. "I'll call the sheriff when we get back to my place. He can't accuse me of seeking attention. He needs to know about this—he's still looking for those involved in Lana's death."

"He can't prove a crime. A grown woman has a right to refuse medical care. And she probably did refuse at first. Members of the Vine are taught that relying on outside care is a sign of weak faith. No one wants to be accused of that."

She turned and began walking back down the way they had come. This glimpse of the Vine—or what she thought was the Vine—had changed the mood of the day. Chris now walked with her head down and shoulders bowed, unspeaking.

He wanted to tell her to cheer up. She wasn't part of the group anymore, and they had no hold on her. But he dismissed the impulse as soon as it surfaced. Some of the members of that group had knocked him out and broken into her home. They had threatened her verbally and physically. She had every right to be afraid and to wonder if she would ever be rid of them.

So he settled for moving up beside her on the trail. "It may not feel like it, but you've got a lot of friends in this town," he said. "Every member of search and rescue would help you if you asked. Jasmine thinks of you like a daughter. Bethany thinks you're a superhero—and she wouldn't be wrong. And of course, there's me."

She glanced up at him. "And what are you?"

"I'm just someone who likes being with you," he said. "I'm the one who'll break the trail ahead or stand by your side or watch your back. Whatever you need."

She didn't answer right away. He started to ask if he had overwhelmed her with bad-romance dialogue when she said, "I've never had anyone to do those things before. I'm usually charting my own path."

"I'm not stopping you," he said. "I just want you to know I'm here. If you need me."

She straightened. "And what's in it for you, Doctor?"

He flashed his most insolent grin. "I get to hang out with a hot younger woman. It does wonders for my image, I tell you."

As he had hoped, she burst out laughing, then punched his shoulder. He laughed too. "For that, I think you owe me dinner," she said.

It's a date, he thought. But no, he wouldn't use the D word. He didn't want to scare her off. "That's a great idea." He hooked his thumbs beneath the straps of his pack. "First one down gets to pick the restaurant." Then he set off, long strides eating up the distance.

"That's not fair. You have longer legs than me," she called.

"What was that? I'm an old man, remember? I'm probably losing my hearing."

He was still enjoying her laughter when she blew past him, shoes raising puffs of dust as she raced down the trail.

Nineteen years ago

"Mom! Mom! Peace and Victory and I were playing by the creek, and we saw the biggest fish!" Elita skidded to a stop in the middle of the trailer's main room and stared at the boxes stacked around the room. "What's going on?"

Her mother looked up from one of the boxes. "We're moving. Come on. You can help me wrap these dishes." She indicated the stack of plates on the coffee table beside her.

"Why do we have to move?" Elita stamped her foot. "I like it here." There were the woods to play in and the little creek, and the secret playhouse she and her friends had made with sticks and vines in a spot no one knew about but them.

"The Exalted says it's time to move, so we're moving." Mom didn't look any happier about the relocation than Elita.

"We're moving to an even better location." Her father

came into the room, carrying the stack of old blankets they used to cushion fragile items for the move.

"How do you know that?" her mother asked. "This was supposed to be a better location, too, but we've only been here six months, and already we have to move."

"The Exalted said it's not fertile ground," her father said.

"Is he planting a garden?" Elita asked. Some of their neighbors had little gardens planted around their tents or trailers. Elita and her friends sometimes dug in the dirt and "planted" flowers and twigs and things. She liked playing in the cool dirt.

"He means there aren't many people around here who want to learn the Exalted's teachings." Her dad patted her head.

"Or maybe the locals have complained about us squatting here," her mother said.

Her father's expression darkened. "Don't let anyone hear you say that," he said. "If people really understood the gift the Exalted could give them, they would welcome us with open arms and beg us to stay as long as possible so they could hear his teachings."

Her mother bent over the dishes again, shaking her head. "There are some old newspapers in the kitchen, Elita," she said. "Would you get them for me?"

She had just picked up the stack of papers when someone knocked on the back door. She walked over and opened it, and stared, open mouthed, at the man who stood there. The man—tall and broad shouldered, with a mop of blond hair and piercing blue eyes—stared back at her. He reminded Elita of a picture of Jack in the copy of *Jack and the Beanstalk* her mother had read to her. "Hello, Elita," the man said. "Is your father here?"

"How did you know my name?" she asked.

"I know all about you," the man said. "The Exalted has asked me to keep an eye on you. You're a lucky girl to be so fated."

"Jedediah! What can I do for you?" Her father hurried to greet the man.

"You need to be ready to head out by one o'clock," Jedediah said. "Cephus will be here then to tow your trailer. You and your family will travel in the bus."

"I don't want to move," Elita said.

Both men turned to her. "Elita, hush!" her father ordered. "It's not your place to question the Exalted."

"Your father is right," Jedediah said. "Your job is to obey. The sooner you master that job, the better for you and for the group. No supper for you tonight, to teach you to master your impulses."

He exited the trailer, and Elita began to cry. Her mother came into the room. "What's going on? Elita, why are you crying?"

"Jedediah was here," her father said. "Elita told him she didn't want to move. He said for questioning the Exalted, she was forbidden to have supper tonight."

"Who is he to tell us how to discipline our daughter?" Her mother put an arm around Elita. "And she's only eight."

Her father looked troubled. "We can't disobey Jedediah," he said. "He's the Exalted's right-hand man."

"I'm not going to starve my child."

"She won't starve. She's gone longer than one night without food during the ritual fasts."

"And you know I don't agree with those either. Not for children."

Her father glanced out the window. "Lower your voice.

Someone will hear you. And get back to packing. They're coming for the trailer at one." The family didn't own a truck, so they relied on one of the other members of the Vine to tow their travel trailer to the next camp. They would ride with other families in a converted school bus the group owned.

Chris's mother frowned at her husband, then marched to the cabinet and took out bread and peanut butter. "What are you doing?" her father asked.

"I'm making a sandwich."

"You can't give it to Elita."

"The sandwich is for me." She spread peanut butter between two slices of bread, then wrapped it in wax paper and tucked it in her pocket. As she exited the room, she caught Elita's eye and winked. Elita immediately felt better. Later on, when no one was looking, she knew her mother would give her the sandwich. Her father might believe in strict obedience to the Exalted, but her mother had different priorities, and Elita was one of them.

Chapter Thirteen

Rand was off work the next day and spent the morning doing yard work around the cabin while Chris worked on a new painting on the screened-in porch she had appropriated as a temporary studio. Every time he passed by, he looked up to see her poised before an easel, sometimes working with a brush or pencil, other times standing back and considering the work so far.

He could get used to her presence in his life, though he wanted more. An intimacy she wasn't ready to give and a trust he didn't know if he could ever earn.

He had just fetched a can of wasp spray from the garage to deal with a yellow jacket nest under the back deck when his phone emitted an alert. He checked the screen and found a message from the 911 dispatcher: Missing hikers, Guthrie Mill area. All available volunteers needed for search.

He went inside, still carrying the spray. He set the can on the counter and went in search of Chris. She had laid aside her paintbrush and was staring at her phone also. "Where is Guthrie Mill?" he asked.

She pocketed her phone. "It's an old stamp mill for processing gold ore in the mountains, about ten thousand feet in elevation," she said. "It's south of Gallagher's Basin."

"That's not far from where we were hiking yesterday."

"Not far as the crow flies," she said. "A lot longer if you travel by road. It's a beautiful area but a terrible place to be lost. Lots of hazards."

Rand thought of the first search and rescue training class he had attended, about the psychology of searches. "Let's hope we can find these people before they get into trouble," he said.

"I'll get my gear," she said, and left the room.

They met up at the front door a few moments later and rode together to search and rescue headquarters, where a crowd had gathered of both SAR volunteers and others who had gotten word of the need for searchers. "The 911 call came in at ten this morning," Danny said when the SAR team gathered around him. "Two adults—a husband and wife in their forties, and their fifteen-year-old son. They set out two days ago to explore the area around Guthrie Mill. The neighbors noticed this morning they hadn't returned and became concerned and made the call."

"Are we sure they're really missing?" Ryan asked. "Maybe they took off somewhere else and didn't bother informing their neighbor of the change of plans."

"The caller was insistent that something was wrong," Danny said. "He said none of the family members were answering their phones and the husband was supposed to report for work this morning and didn't. He also said the boy is a diabetic and needs regular insulin."

"Do we know their names?" Sheri asked.

"The caller referred to the man as Mike and the son as AJ," Danny said. "The woman is Ruth. No last names. And the caller lost the connection before giving his own information. The 911 operator said the connection was poor, and the caller spoke with a thick accent she had trouble understanding. She thinks his name was Morris or Maurice, but the call dropped before she was able to get more information. She thought maybe he had driven into the mountains to look for the family. His phone didn't register with the 911 system."

"That's a little suspicious," Chris said.

"Maybe," Danny said. "But bad phone service is pretty common in these mountains and canyons. We can't risk ignoring this in case it is legitimate. That area around the mill is particularly hazardous. There are open pits, collapsing structures and rusting equipment."

"That kid could be in trouble if he needs insulin," Hannah said.

"The sheriff's department is looking for vehicles at trailheads in the area that might belong to this family," Danny continued. "They've asked us to begin our search at the mill and move outward. We'll work in teams of four."

Rand and Chris teamed up with Carrie Andrews and Caleb Garrison. "We're supposed to focus from the area south of the mill to Raccoon Creek." Caleb looked up from the map the group had been given. "Are any of you familiar with the area?"

"I am," Carrie and Chris replied at the same time.

"I've been to the mill a couple of times but not recently," Caleb said.

"I've never been there," Rand admitted.

"Just follow us." Carrie stashed the map in her pack. "Let's go, and hope we can find this lost family."

ONLY THE SHELL of the Guthrie Mill remained—the weathered wooden walls, three stories high, topped by a metal roof streaked with orange rust. Light streamed through gaps in the boards, and the whole structure leaned a foot to the left, the victim of almost a century of punishing winds and deep winter snows. The ground around the structure was a junkyard of splintered boards and rusting metal, the husk of a boiler, snarls of thick cable, discarded tin cans, and the remnants of the iron rails that had once been a path for ore cars bringing raw materials for the mill to process.

Chris was drawn to places like this, and she had painted many similar scenes. Wildflowers grew among the debris, bending in a stiff breeze, and fluffy clouds scudded by in a delft-blue sky. It was the perfect setting for a summer outing—and a terrible place to be lost. The ground sloped away on all sides into deep ravines and rock-filled gullies, rock uplifts, and the remnants of other buildings that had supported the mill's operation, making it impossible to see clearly for more than a few dozen yards in any direction. "When was the last time you were up here?" Rand asked as the four searchers picked their way over the rough ground.

"Harley and I were up here last summer," Chris said. "I had an idea for a new painting and spent a couple of hours poking around and making sketches. We were the only ones here that afternoon."

"Did you complete the painting?" he asked.

"I did. It sold right away. To a woman from Cincinnati, I think." She scanned the surroundings for any clue that someone else had passed by here recently—a torn bit of clothing, a food wrapper, debris that appeared disturbed—but saw nothing.

"What are we supposed to be looking for?" Rand asked. "Besides the obvious, a person or persons?"

"Look for anything that could have attracted someone off the trail," Chris said.

"They might have followed the old tramway" Carrie said. She indicated the remains of the towers evenly spaced across the mountain. "There's a lot of old cable and tram cars beneath the towers that interest people. And a lot of rough terrain where someone could fall or get hurt."

"Then let's follow the tramline," Caleb said.

They set out along the tramline, but Chris had trouble focusing on the search. She couldn't shake the sense that something wasn't right. Why had the 911 caller provided so many specific details—the family's destination and the fact that the boy had diabetes—but failed to lead with important information, such as the family's name or his own contact info? And if the family had really been gone for two days, why hadn't a relative or coworker reported them missing?

She reminded herself that it wasn't her job to raise suspicions about the call. She was here to search for people who might be in trouble and to help them if they were found. If they were all wasting their time, there were worse ways to spend a summer afternoon than in this beautiful spot.

A delicate melody, like someone playing a flute, drifted to her. Was that music or a trick of the wind? She stopped.

Ahead of her, Rand stopped also. "What is it?" he asked.

She shook her head. "I thought I heard music."

"I don't hear anything," Caleb said.

"Which direction was it coming from?" Rand asked.

"I don't know. Let's keep going." She was freaking herself out, hearing things that weren't there. Better to focus on the search.

They hadn't gone much farther when Caleb halted. "I thought I saw movement over there." He pointed to a copse of stunted pinions.

"Yes." Chris leaned forward. "A flash of blue—like

a shirt or something." She had just glimpsed the motion through the trees, the brightness of the blue out of place amid the greens and browns of the landscape.

"Is it another searcher?" Rand asked.

"No one else is assigned to this sector." Carrie started forward.

They all followed. Chris was at the back of the line, and kept looking toward the trees. *There!* She had seen the flash of color again.

Then she heard the music once more. A high-pitched melody. She stopped, but the others kept going, intent on reaching the trees. She tried to figure out where the music was coming from. Back the way they had come and to the left. She just needed to get close enough to verify there was really someone there.

She took a few steps off the trail, keeping the others in sight. She would check this out, then catch back up with them to report. Abruptly, the music stopped, replaced by a voice: "Help!" The sound was faint and high pitched. A woman, or maybe a child.

Heart pounding, she broke into a trot, moving toward the sound. "Hello?" she called. "Is someone there?"

Something landed on her head, covering her face. She clawed at the rough cloth, but someone grabbed her hands. She tried to cry out, but her voice was barely audible. And then there was nothing but darkness.

CARRIE STOPPED AGAIN and stared intently ahead of them. Rand stood beside her. "There's definitely someone up there," he said.

"I see them." Carrie took off again at a jog. "Hey!" she shouted. "We're with search and rescue!"

"Why are they running away?" Caleb asked. He caught up with Rand and Carrie. The person they had been pursuing had disappeared behind a grouping of boulders.

"Stop!" Carrie called. "We need to talk to you."

"Where did they go?" Caleb asked. "I don't see them."

Rand looked back over his shoulder, expecting to see Chris hurrying to catch up with them. Instead, there was no one there. "Where's Chris?" he asked.

Carrie stopped. "She was right behind us."

"Chris!" Rand listened for a response but heard nothing. He cupped his hands around his mouth and shouted again: "Chris!"

"Caleb, wait!" Carrie called. "We can't find Chris."

Caleb jogged back to them. "I can't find whoever we saw up there either." He removed his cap and wiped the sweat from his forehead. "What happened to Chris?"

"I don't know." Rand started back the way they had come. "Chris!" he shouted. Fear constricted his chest, making it hard to breathe. He searched the ground for any sign of a scuffle, but the hard surface showed no footprints or indications of a disturbance.

Carrie took out her radio. "The sheriff's department is supposed to have a drone up to help with the search," she said. "I'll ask them to head this way, see if they can spot Chris."

"How could she have just disappeared?" Caleb asked. "And where did that guy we were chasing vanish to?"

"I think he lured us away on purpose," Rand said.

Caleb frowned. "Why would he do that?"

"So that someone else could grab Chris." He scanned the empty landscape, seeing nothing but mining ruins, rocks and a distant bank of dark clouds in the distance. Rain was coming, though it wasn't here yet. "The Vine didn't leave the county after all. Yesterday Chris and I hiked the Blue Sky Trail, and we spotted some campers across the valley that we thought might be them. I meant to report the sighting to the sheriff but never got the chance. The story about the missing family may have been a ruse to get us up here to the mill so they could snatch her." A cold knot in the pit of his stomach told him he was right.

Carrie ended her call. "Danny wants us to report back to the trailhead. They're calling off the search."

"Why are they calling it off?" Caleb asked.

Carrie shrugged. "Not sure. He just said to meet at the trailhead."

"Did you let him know Chris is missing?" Rand asked.

"I did. He says we need to talk to the sheriff. They need coordinates to pinpoint the search." She clapped Rand on the back. "Let's go. The sooner we tell them what we know, the sooner they can find her."

"You two go on to the trailhead," Rand said. "I'll stay here."

"No way," Caleb said. "First rule of working in the wilderness is you don't split up."

"Something must have distracted Chris, or she would have remembered that," Carrie said.

Rand wanted to know what that something was. He thought about arguing with the others, but that was delaying the search. He took out his phone and called up a mapping app to pinpoint their location. He would come back here—with or without the others. He wasn't going to abandon Chris.

"WE'VE CALLED OFF the search because we've determined the call was a hoax," Sheriff Travis Walker addressed the crowd of searchers gathered at the Guthrie Mill trailhead. "We haven't identified anyone who fits the description the caller gave, the phone itself was a temporary 'burner' phone purchased at the local gas station by someone the clerk could only describe as 'an average-looking, middle-aged white male.' We haven't located any vehicles left overnight at any of the trailheads, not just in the area of the mill but anywhere in the county. We have issued a plea for any information from anyone who might know the family described or the person who called in the report, but at this time we feel there's too great a risk that someone else will be hurt while searching for someone we can't be satisfied even exists."

"What about Chris Mercer's disappearance?" Rand asked. "What are you doing about that?"

"We're sending up a drone to survey the area where she went missing, and we're enlisting search and rescue to assist in a targeted search for her." Travis scanned the faces of those around him. "I know you're concerned that one of your own is missing," he said. "I promise, we're doing everything in our power to locate her. She is our number one priority."

"Search and rescue has a search dog, right?" Rand remembered meeting the woman who had trained the dog—Anna something.

"Anna and Jacquie are away for the week doing a course for an additional certification," Danny said. "By the time we got another dog and handler here, the rain would have degraded any scent trail."

At his words, Rand and several others looked up at the dark clouds moving toward them. "Can you think of anything else that would help us find her?" Travis asked.

"Chris and I hiked the Blue Sky Trail yesterday," Rand said. "We spotted some campers across the valley. We thought it might be some of the members of the Vine. I meant to call and tell you about it this morning, but I forgot." He had been too distracted by his new closeness with Chris to want to think about the Vine.

"Do you have coordinates for this camp?" Travis asked.

"We were standing at the top of the ridge at the end of the trail, looking south."

Deputy Dwight Prentice approached. "Sheriff, if I could speak to you for a moment."

Travis moved away with Dwight. Rand followed, listening in on their conversation while trying to appear uninterested. "Wes has located a group of campers with the drone," Dwight said. "They have a couple of tents set up in the next basin over from the mill. There's no sign of Chris Mercer or of anyone fitting the description of the supposed missing family."

Travis looked back at Rand. "How many people were in this camp you and Chris saw from the Blue Sky Trail?" he asked.

"There were over a dozen small tents and several large ones," he said. "Easily a couple of dozen people of all ages."

"The drone reported only a couple of tents and five or six people," Dwight said.

"And where are they, exactly?" Travis asked.

Dwight consulted his notebook. "A basin to the west of Guthrie Mill, next to a big outcropping of rock."

"That's a different area than the one Chris and I were looking into," Rand said.

"Let's talk to these people anyway," Travis said. "Maybe they've seen or heard something." He keyed his radio microphone and told Wes to keep searching with the drone. "Dwight, come with me to talk to these campers."

Rand moved forward. "I want to come too."

"No," Travis said.

"I've spent more time in the Vine's camp than anyone else here except Danny," Rand said. "I'll recognize if these campers are part of the group."

"Why do you think the Vine is involved?" Travis asked.

"Because Chris is missing. The group has been hunting her for fifteen years, and they've already tried to take her once recently. I'm sure they had something to do with her disappearance."

Travis and Dwight exchanged a look Rand interpreted as skeptical. "You can't come with us," Travis said.

"Then I'll follow you up there."

"I could have you detained for interfering with an investigation."

"What would that do but create more paperwork and hassle for you?" Rand did his best to look calm and nonthreatening even though inside, this waste of time chafed. "I promise I'll stay out of the way. But you'll have a third set of eyes on hand to watch these people while you question them."

Travis fixed him with a hard stare, but Rand didn't relent. The sheriff was the first to blink. "You can come with us," he said. "But you'll stay back, follow orders and keep quiet."

"Yes, sir."

Travis and Dwight collected packs from their cruiser and set out up the trail to the mill, Rand following behind. None of them spoke for the first mile; then Travis glanced back at Rand. "How long have you known Chris?" he asked.

"A few weeks."

"And you believe what she's told you about this group, the Vine?"

"Yes. You heard that man on the trail the day Chris and I met—the one who told her to get ready for her wedding."

"People with mistaken beliefs or delusions aren't necessarily threatening," Travis said.

"She said the Vine killed her father when he opposed their leader."

"She was a child. Maybe he really did eat poisonous mushrooms."

"I believe Chris. And she didn't make up the two men who attacked me and broke into her apartment. What I saw when Danny and I went to the camp fit with her description of the group."

Travis nodded. "Tell me again what happened when she disappeared this morning."

Rand repeated the story of seeing someone moving ahead and going to investigate. "Chris was bringing up the rear of the group. I was focused on whoever was ahead of us and didn't notice she had fallen farther behind. When I did look back, she was gone."

"What do you think happened?" Travis asked.

"I think you're right about the missing persons call being a hoax. I think whoever called in that story did so to lure search and rescue into the area around the mill. They knew Chris was likely to respond to the call."

"They couldn't be sure she would volunteer to be part of the search," Dwight said.

"If she didn't, they didn't lose anything," Rand said.

"They took a big chance," Travis said. "The area around the mill was crawling with searchers."

"It's a big area," Rand said. "Even with so many people

searching, we were spread out. And there's a lot of cover up there—rocks, clumps of trees, old mine buildings and the changing terrain itself."

"Maybe she fell and was injured," Dwight said.

That was a possibility Rand had considered. "Why didn't we hear her cry out?"

"Maybe you were too far away," Dwight said. "Or she lost consciousness."

"Maybe." Rand didn't like to think Chris had been hurt, but if the injury wasn't serious, wouldn't that be better than being back in the clutches of the Vine? "Is the drone still looking for her?" he asked.

"It is," the sheriff said. "And I spoke with Danny. There's a new team of searchers headed up right behind us."

After three miles and an hour of steady hiking, they reached the mill. Dwight checked the coordinates he had received from the drone. "Looks like we head this way," he said, and pointed toward the same copse of trees where Rand and his group of searchers had seen someone running away from them.

They passed through the trees and hiked for another forty-five minutes before they spotted two tents—one orange and one lime green—set in a broad bowl on the side of the mountain. As they drew nearer, Rand counted five people, all adults, moving among the tents. Backpacks and other camping gear had been arranged near a fire ring.

Two young couples made up the group. A slender man in his twenties, with straight dark hair and glasses, moved forward. He focused on Dwight's and Travis's uniforms. "Is something wrong?" he asked.

"We're looking for a missing woman," Travis said.

"Midtwenties, five foot six, medium build, shoulder-length blue hair."

The man shook his head. "We haven't seen anyone like that." The second man and the two women, who had gathered around him, shook their heads also.

Travis looked around at the tents and other gear. The tents were small—not the place to hide someone. "How long have you been camping here?" Travis asked.

"We set up last night. It's okay to be camped here, isn't it?"

"It's not illegal to camp here," Travis said.

Something rustled in the trees, and Rand glanced over in time to see a dark-haired girl step into the clearing. At the sight of Travis and the others, she started and moved back into the cover of the leaves. "Who was that?" Travis asked.

"That's my niece," the second man, a broad-shouldered blond, said. "She's very shy."

Rand stared after the girl. "Ask her to come back," he said. "I want to talk to her."

"Who are you?" the first man asked.

Travis sent Rand a quelling look. "Can your niece answer a few questions for us?" the sheriff asked.

"You won't get anything useful from her," the second man said. "She's got the mental capacity of a three-year-old. A sad situation, really."

"I'd still like to talk to her," Travis said.

The two men looked at each other. "I'm going to have to refuse," the blond said. "No disrespect, Sheriff, but I don't see any need to upset her. She couldn't tell you anything useful."

Silence stretched as Travis and the blond faced each other; then the sheriff took a step back. "We'll be back if we have more questions," he said.

Rand waited until they were a quarter mile from camp before he burst out. "I know that girl," he said. "She was in the Vine's camp the night Danny and I tried to help that pregnant woman, Lana. They called her Serena. And she seemed as smart as any ten- or eleven-year-old."

"If they've got Chris, she isn't in that camp," Dwight said. "I got a good look at the tents. They're so small I don't think they could hide anyone in them."

"She's probably in the woods," Rand said. "Wherever the girl was coming from. That's why they didn't want us talking to her."

"Or they might not want strangers interviewing a child," Dwight said.

"We'll get searchers up here," Travis said. "It's public land. They can't stop us from searching."

"And while we're waiting, they'll move Chris," Rand said. He turned back toward the camp. "I'm going back there to look for Chris myself."

"Don't do it," Travis said.

Rand made a move to turn away, but Dwight took hold of his arm. "Don't do anything rash," Dwight said. "You're not going to face off by yourself against four of them, and who knows how many more? If they do have Chris, they probably have her guarded. Smarter to let us check out the situation with a drone and get back up there with the numbers to deal with whatever kind of offense they try to present."

Rand glanced at Travis. "We may not have a lot of time," he said. "Groups like this are used to moving around a lot, avoiding any attention from police."

"We're wasting time right now," Travis said. "Don't delay us any longer."

Rand glanced back over his shoulder. He wanted to go

back and look for Chris, but he could see the foolishness of trying to take on the group by himself, unarmed. "All right," he said. "I'll wait." But he wouldn't wait long.

Chapter Fourteen

Chris woke up with a pounding head, the pain worse than any tension headache or hangover she had ever experienced. She forced open her eyes and was met with a wave of nausea, and she broke into a cold sweat. "Drink this. It will help." A gentle, cool hand briefly rested on her forehead, and the hand's owner, a dark-haired girl, helped Chris sit up against some rough surface. She pressed a mug into Chris's hands. "Don't worry. It's just ginger tea. It will help, I promise."

Chris sipped the drink, which indeed tasted of ginger and smelled of lemons and honey. She realized suddenly how parched she was and ended up draining the cup. The girl smiled and took the cup from her. "That's good. You should feel better soon."

The only light in the dim space was from an old-fashioned camping lantern, which gave off an erratic yellow glow and the faint odor of gas. Chris shoved herself up into a sitting position, fighting a new wave of dizziness and nausea. She had been lying—and was now sitting—on what appeared to be an old sleeping bag laid out on the floor of a chamber hewed out of rock. The entrance wasn't visible from where she sat, but a draft of fresh air to her left probably came from that opening. "Where am I?" she asked.

"We're in a cave, I think. Or maybe something to do with one of the mines around here." The girl set the empty cup aside and picked up a basin filled with water. "Let me look at the back of your head. I want to make sure the bleeding has stopped."

Most of her fogginess had cleared, and the memory of what had happened on the trail returned, sharp and enraging. Chris leaned away from the girl. "Who are you? Why am I here?"

"My name is Serena." The girl's expression was guarded. Unsmiling. Nevertheless, she was strikingly beautiful. She had the kind of arresting beauty that might grace magazine covers or classical paintings. "And we are both here because the Exalted wills it."

Of course. Chris hadn't really had to ask the question. The Exalted was the only person who would want to kidnap her. "You're a member of the Vine," she clarified.

Serena dipped a cloth into the water and wrung it out. "I was born into the Vine."

"How old are you?"

"I'm ten."

"Who else is here?" Chris looked around the cave. Anything more than a few feet from the lantern's flame was pitch black, but it didn't feel as if anyone else was nearby.

"There is a guard outside the entrance. Probably several guards. Please, let me look at your injury."

Chris hesitated, then turned her back to the girl. Serena was so slight that even in her injured state, Chris felt sure she could defend herself against the child if necessary.

"I'm going to clean away some of the dried blood in your hair," Serena said.

Chris winced as the cool water—or maybe the soap in

it—stung the gash on her head. "That was a nasty fall you took," Serena said as she dabbed at the wound. "You must have hit a big rock."

"I didn't fall," Chris said. "Someone hit me, though maybe they used a rock."

"Who would do that?" Serena asked.

Chris didn't answer. How could she explain anything to this child?

Heavy bootheels striking rock echoed around them. Serena's hand stilled, and Chris turned to see Jedediah. The lantern's flickering flame cast macabre shadows over his face, deepening every crag and crevice, turning his eyes to dark smudges and highlighting his large yellowing teeth. "Good, you're awake," he said.

"She said she didn't fall," Serena said. "Someone hit her in the head."

Jedediah didn't look at the girl. "She's confused. She fell."

"I didn't fall until someone hit me." Chris wanted to stand up to face him, but she was afraid if she did so, she might faint. She had to settle for glaring up at him. "You can't keep me here. People will be looking for me."

"They won't find you."

"Where am I?" She didn't remember any caves in the area around Guthrie Mill, but there were plenty of old mines.

"It doesn't matter," he said. "We're not going to stay here long. We're moving you to a new hiding place right away. By tomorrow you'll be halfway across the country." He turned to Serena. "Get her dressed in those clothes I left. And don't forget the wig."

He left, his footsteps echoing behind him. Serena moved

to Chris's side, a bundle of fabric in one hand, a curly blond wig in the other. "You need to put these on," she said. "I can help you if you're still feeling dizzy."

Chris eyed the long-sleeved dress, with its high neckline and long skirt, and the blond wig. "Why do I have to wear those things?" she asked, even though she thought she knew the answer. Once she put on that outfit, no one would be able to see her tattoos or blue hair—the very things anyone searching for her would be looking for.

"I don't know." Serena thrust them at her again. "The Exalted wills it."

This was the reasoning given for any number of actions within the Vine, from a designated fasting day to a dictate of what clothing people would wear, to the decision to move to a new location. Chris eyed the dress—a particularly drab shade of faded gray. "I won't wear any of that," she said.

Serena bit her lower lip. "If you don't put them on, they'll punish you," she said.

"I'm not afraid of their punishment." Not entirely true, but right now she was too angry to pay much attention to the fear lurking at the back of her throat.

"They'll punish me too." The words came out as a whisper, but they stung like a scream. The child had been hurt before.

"Where are your parents?" Chris asked.

"My parents have gone on to glory," she answered, blurting the statement like a child reciting the multiplication tables.

The familiar phrase sent another chill through Chris. "Do you mean they're dead?" she asked. "Both of them?"

Serena nodded. "Please put the clothing on," she said.

"All right."

Serena—who was strong despite her slight frame— helped Chris stand. "Do you need help undressing?" she asked.

"I'll just put this on over my old clothes." Before the girl could protest, Chris slipped the dress over her head. Burlap sacks had more shape than this piece of clothing, Chris decided. "Do you know where we're going?" she asked.

Serena fussed with the tie at the back of the dress. Chris thought she wasn't going to answer, but after a moment she spoke very softly. "I wasn't supposed to hear, but Jedediah said something earlier about a helicopter flying in to take you and the Exalted to a safe place."

"A helicopter?"

"Yes. The Exalted flies in one sometimes."

This was certainly a step up from Edmund Harrison's mode of transportation back when Chris and her mother were part of his followers. Then again, he had been collecting money from his acolytes for a long time. Enough, apparently, to pay for a private helicopter. If he took Chris away in that, her friends would have a very difficult time locating her.

Before she could prod the girl for more details, Jedediah returned with three other men. "We need to go now." He took Chris's arm. One of the other three took hold of Serena. "Don't try to fight," Jedediah said. "If you do, we'll hurt the girl."

The look in his eyes made her believe he would enjoy doing so. She bowed her head and meekly went with him. But inside, she was seething, her mind furiously searching for some way out of the mess.

She was startled to find it was almost dark out, the sun only a lavender afterglow above the mountains, the air cool despite her layers of clothing. It would be full dark soon, an inky blackness without the benefit of light from buildings or cars or streetlights. The kind of darkness in which a person could step off a cliff and never know it until they were falling.

The guard's headlamps lit the way up the trail. The group climbed higher, up into the mountains. Were they taking her to a place where the helicopter could land and pick her up? It seemed very late in the day for that. If walking in the mountains after dark was dangerous, flying then presented a host of other hazards. The rescue helicopters they sometimes used needed daylight for their maneuvers.

They stopped before what was clearly a mine entrance, complete with a massive iron gate designed to keep out treasure hunters who might end up falling down a shaft or crushed by collapsing rock or drowned in flooded tunnels. Jedediah pulled open the gate and shoved hard at Chris's back so that she stumbled forward. Serena was pushed in after her, and the gate clanged shut. Jedediah fitted a heavy chain and a brass lock to the entrance. "You can't break the lock," he said. "Don't waste time trying. And we won't be far away."

They left, and Serena began to sob. Chris put her arms around the girl and tried to comfort her even as she fought her own fear. "It's going to be okay," she whispered. "I have a lot of friends looking for me."

"Are the police your friends?" Serena asked.

"Yes." At least, Chris was sure law enforcement would be part of the search. The sheriff and the deputies she knew were friendly and good at their job, even if she wasn't close to them. She wasn't really close to anyone other than her mother.

And Rand. She was beginning to feel close to him. Surely he would be looking for her.

"I saw two men in uniform with guns," Serena said. "I came to the camp where Jedediah had sent a few of us. I wanted to get water for you, and the ginger tea. The two uniformed men and a third man with them saw me. That made the others angry at me. They told me it wasn't smart of me to let the lawmen see me."

"You are smart," Chris said. "I had only known you a few minutes before I figured that out. And it's good that the officers saw you." And the third man—had that been Rand? "That means they were close. They'll keep looking for us."

"How will they find us now that we've moved?"

They had probably been moved in order to get farther away from the searchers. "Search and rescue has a dog that can follow people's scents and find them," Chris said. She had marveled at how adept fellow SAR volunteer Anna Trent's standard poodle, Jacquie, was at locating lost and missing people.

"A dog?" Serena sounded skeptical.

"It doesn't matter how they find us," Chris said. "I know they won't give up until they do." And Chris wouldn't give up either. She would find a way to fight back. She would follow her mother's example and do whatever it took to break free of the Vine once again.

DESPITE RAND'S DETERMINATION to search for Chris all night if necessary, he was sent home as darkness fell. Danny had cornered him as he prepared to set out with a new group of volunteers who planned to focus around the area where he and Travis and Dwight had interviewed the campers. "Go home," Danny said. "You're dead on your feet, and you're going to end up hurt and we'll have to rescue you too." Before Rand could protest, he added, "I haven't announced it yet, but we're pulling in all the searchers. It's not safe to have people up on the mountains after dark. Try to get some rest, and we'll start up in the morning."

Rand wanted to protest that he could keep going. He'd be careful, stick to known trails and use his headlamp. But he saw the wisdom in Danny's words. The chances of finding Chris in the dark were minuscule, and the odds of himself or someone with him getting hurt increased with the loss of daylight.

When he unlocked his door, he was greeted by Harley, who howled and sniffed him all over, then gave him what seemed to Rand a reproachful look. "I'm sorry, but she's not with me," he said, rubbing the dog's ears. "I promise we're going to find her soon." He hoped that was a promise he could keep.

He fed the dog and forced himself to eat a ham sandwich. He should take a shower and go to bed, but he was too agitated. He riffled through his collection of hiking maps and found one for the area around Guthrie Mill and spread it on the table. While Harley watched from his dog bed in the corner, Rand studied the map. He circled the spot where he thought the campers he had visited today had been with a yellow highlighter, then chose a blue marker to inscribe a circle around this spot. At least half the circle was occupied by a rocky couloir falling away from a 13,000-foot peak that was unnamed on the map. Hard to get to for searchers, but also for anyone trying to hide Chris.

That left the rest of the area encompassed by the circle—a network of abandoned mines, lesser peaks and high mountain meadows. Chris could be anywhere in this area.

There were no roads up there, so the only way to get her away from the trail near the mill where they had taken her was to walk. And they would be able to walk only so far in the approximately six hours since they had kidnapped her. Darkness would halt their progress, just as it had the progress of searchers. Or at least, it would slow them down, if they were foolish enough to try to traverse the terrain by starlight. So the odds were high that she was still in the area within that blue circle.

Harley followed Rand into his bedroom, where he filled his pack with extra clothing and first aid supplies. Then the two of them went into the kitchen, where Rand packed food and water. He glanced at the dog, then stuck in packets of canine food and biscuits. Harley wasn't a trained tracker, but he was devoted to Chris. Rand counted on the dog to home in on any scent of her.

Lastly, he returned to the bedroom and unlocked the safe where he kept the sidearm he had owned since his days in the service. He had no doubt the members of the Vine were armed, and he wanted to be prepared.

Only then did he take a shower and go to bed. He set his alarm for an hour before sunrise. At first light, he and Harley would be back at the spot where he had seen the girl, Serena, emerging from the woods. The girl was part of the Vine. Following her should lead him to the group and—he hoped—to Chris.

CHRIS COULDN'T SLEEP. Her head pounded and her stomach churned. Everywhere she tried to sit or lie was uncomfortable. Her stomach growled, and she realized she hadn't eaten since breakfast. And what about the girl? "Are they not going to feed us?" she asked.

"I guess not." Serena sat nearby, close enough that Chris could hear her breathing. "The Exalted says fasting is good for purifying one's thoughts."

It was another one of those things members of the Vine said, parroting their leader. Chris had said those things, too, when she was a child, trying to please the adults around her and not stand out from the group. She couldn't say if she had actually believed those things, having become part of the group when she was five. But Serena had been taught these lessons since birth. That was the only reality she knew—a frightening thought itself.

"Come sit beside me," she said, and patted the ground next to her.

Serena slid over, and Chris put an arm around her. "I lived with the Vine when I was your age," she said. "My father died. They said it was from eating poisonous mushrooms. After that, my mother decided she and I should leave the group."

She waited for Serena to express the usual horror that anyone would leave the Exalted and his teachings. How could someone give up the chance for new life on a higher plane? How could they sacrifice the opportunity for true enlightenment and rejoin an evil and dangerous world?

"I never knew anyone who left," Serena said. She cuddled closer to Chris's side. "I mean, I've heard people whisper about ones who left, but they were just…gone. No one ever heard from them again."

"I never knew anyone who left either," Chris admitted. She knew there were others who had escaped, and her mother remembered some of the names. But they never met any former members out in the "real" world. Had some of them, like her father, been eliminated at the Exalted's orders? Was it possible she and her mother were the only ones who got away, and that was part of the reason for the Exalted's dogged pursuit? "What happened to your parents?" she asked.

"Something was wrong with the heater in our trailer, and they went to sleep and never woke up," Serena said.

"Do you mean carbon monoxide poisoning?"

"Yes, I think so."

"Where were you when this happened?"

"I was spending the night with Helen. I was eight, and it was supposed to be a special treat."

So Helen was still with the group. "Is Helen your friend?" she asked.

"More of a teacher, I guess."

"Had you spent the night with Helen before?" Chris asked.

"No. This was the first time. We made pizza and played Chinese checkers."

A treat, or a means of getting the little girl out of the way while her parents were gotten rid of? "Where do you live now?"

"With Helen. We have our own trailer, next to the Exalted. I have my own room. Sometimes he comes to visit me. When I'm older, I'm going to marry him. But you're going to marry him first."

A shudder went through Chris. The life Serena was living would have been Chris's life if she and her mother had stayed with the Vine. Chris squeezed the girl's shoulders. She was furious but trying not to show it. Someone had to stop this man, who preyed on innocent children in the name of religion. "I'm not going to marry the Exalted," she said. "I'm going to get away."

"You can't do that. You'll suffer for all eternity."

"Not as much as I'd suffer if I married the Exalted. I'm going to get away."

Serena didn't say anything for so long that Chris thought the child might have fallen asleep. Then she stretched up, her mouth very close to Chris's ear. "When you go, will you take me with you?" she whispered.

Chapter Fifteen

Seven years ago

Chris sat at a coffee shop near the campus of the Rhode Island School of Design, her mocha latte growing cold as she struggled with a sketch of the older woman seated across the room. The deep lines and weathered skin of the woman fascinated Chris, but she was having a hard time conveying the depth and texture to the drawing on the page.

"Do you mind if I sit here? All the other tables are full."

She looked up to see a smiling young man with a mop of sandy curls. She glanced around the room and saw that business had picked up since she had sat down an hour ago, and all the tables were occupied. "Uh, sure." She moved a stack of books over to make more room.

"Thanks." He sat and dropped his backpack on the floor beside his chair. "Are you a student at RIS-D?"

"Yes. Are you?"

He shook his head as he sipped his coffee. "I guess you could say I'm studying philosophy."

"Where are you studying?"

"I'm part of a group led by a fantastic teacher. It's an incredible program. And totally tuition free. I'm learning so much, and it's such a great group of people."

Goose bumps rose along Chris's arms. She closed the sketchbook and slid it into her backpack. "Where is this program?" she asked.

"It's wherever we want it to be. That's the best part. I'm getting this incredible education, for free, and I get to see incredible places like this while I do so."

Providence, Rhode Island, was a nice place, but Chris didn't think it qualified as *incredible*. She reached for the textbooks on the table.

Her table companion put his hand on hers to stop her. "I'll bet you would really like the program I'm in," he said. "Being an artist, you're used to looking at the world with more intention than the average person, am I right? My teacher could show you so much more. It would really enhance your art and your life."

Chris pulled her hand away and picked up the books. The young man's spiel was too familiar, but she needed to find out a little more before she ran away. She needed to know exactly what she was up against. So she forced herself to relax. "What's your teacher's name?" she asked.

"Have you ever heard of a group called the Vine?"

The name sent ice through her, but she somehow managed to remain seated at the table, a pleasant expression on her face. "I don't think so. Is it some kind of winery or something?"

The young man laughed. "Not exactly. It's a group of like-minded people working toward a better world. Our teacher is a tremendous thinker and leader."

"What's his name?" she asked.

The young man sipped his coffee again. "We call him the Exalted. He's just so enlightened. And really caring. I'd like to take you to meet him. You'll be blown away, I promise."

Chris shoved the books into her backpack and stood, almost knocking over her chair in the process. "I just remembered," she said, "I'm late for a class."

She hurried out of the coffee shop and broke into a jog when she reached the sidewalk. The Vine was here, in the smallest state in the union, at a small art school where she happened to be enrolled.

She didn't believe in coincidence. Walking across campus, she pulled out her cell phone and dialed her mother's number.

"Is something wrong?" her mother asked. "You never call me in the middle of the day."

"The Vine is here, in Providence. I just talked to a young man who tried to recruit me."

"Did he know who you are?"

"No. He was just trolling the local coffee shop."

"You need to come home. Now. Before they see you."

"I'll leave this afternoon. As soon as I can pack a few things."

"What will you tell the school?"

"The usual—a family emergency." It wasn't the first time she had left a school or a job suddenly. It was an inconvenience and unfair. But it was better than letting the Vine get her in its clutches again.

THE FIRST RAYS of the sun were burning off the gray of dawn as Rand crouched behind a boulder, looking down on the campsite he and the sheriff and deputy had visited yesterday. He and Harley had been sitting here, cold seeping in, for forty-five minutes, the camp so still he might have thought it abandoned if not for the faint growl of snoring from the closest tent.

He shifted, fighting a cramp in his left thigh, and Harley let out a low whine. Rand froze as two people moved out of the trees, toward the orange tent. He raised his binoculars and recognized Jedediah and an older woman. After a moment, the door to the tent parted, and the younger man with glasses emerged. The three conferred for a moment, then looked up at the sky. Rand followed their gaze and saw a bank of dark clouds moving toward them. A storm would make travel up here more difficult and dangerous, but maybe it would give him and Chris an advantage when it came time to flee. After a moment, Jedediah, the woman and the man from the camp turned and walked back the way they had come.

Rand stowed the binoculars and stood. He picked up the pack, and Harley rose also. "Let's follow them," Rand said.

The dog led the way but stayed close. He had alerted to Rand's wary attitude and followed suit, picking his way carefully over the terrain and keeping silent. Without being told, he set a course that would intersect the route taken by the three they had been watching. When they were near enough to catch a flash of movement in the trees ahead, Rand stopped, and the dog stopped too.

They waited until the trio had passed, then moved forward cautiously, halting every few steps to listen. Rand froze and moved behind a tree when someone—he thought it was Jedediah—spoke, close enough that Rand could understand every word: "Wake up. The helicopter will be here soon, and you need to be ready to go."

Rand didn't hear the answer, but Jedediah and the woman left, leaving the dark-haired man behind, apparently to stand guard.

Harley whined. The hair along the dog's back rose in a

ridge, and he stood stiff-legged, tail and ears alert. "That's where they're holding Chris, isn't it?" Rand said quietly.

He waited until he was sure Jedediah and the woman were gone, then crept closer. He needed to find a way to get rid of the guard without raising an alarm. He watched as the man took a seat on a rock near the mine entrance. He looked disgruntled, pulled from his sleeping bag by Jedediah's early arrival, marched to stand guard without even a cup of coffee.

How to get rid of the man so that Rand could free Chris? He thought back to his military service. He had been a surgeon, not a soldier, but he had heard hundreds of stories from the men and women he cared for, and had seen the results of their efforts on both themselves and the people they fought. The classic approach for dealing with a lone sentry was to sneak up and overpower the guard. Even if the man was only half-awake, Rand didn't see how he could possibly get close enough to do any damage before the guard shouted for help.

A sniper could take him out, but bullets made noise, and Rand wasn't a good enough shot to be sure of hitting the man with a pistol shot from any distance. And the idea of killing someone who had done nothing to harm him repelled him.

He took out his binoculars and scanned the man carefully. If he was armed, the weapon was well hidden. Rand was taller and heavier, so in hand-to-hand combat, he had a good chance of overcoming the guy. He just had to get close enough to launch a surprise attack.

Rustling in the bushes to his right startled him. He turned, one hand on the weapon at his side, in time to see Harley disappearing into the underbrush. He resisted the temptation to call the dog back. What was he doing? This wasn't the time to take off after a rabbit.

"Who's there?"

The guard was staring toward the underbrush where the dog had disappeared. He must have heard the rustling too. The man moved toward the sound. A few more paces and he would be practically on top of Rand. Rand took a careful step back. He started to replace the pistol in its holster, then thought better of it and moved into the underbrush after the dog, both the guard's and the dog's movements helping to drown out any noise he made.

"Who's there?" the guard demanded again. "Come out with your hands up, or I'll shoot."

He's bluffing, Rand thought. The man didn't have a gun. Unless he had drawn one just now. From Rand's position in the clump of scrubby pinion trees, he could see only the side of the man's head. He froze and waited, holding his breath, as the man pushed past him. Then Rand raised his pistol and hit the guard on the back of the head.

The man's legs folded under him, and he toppled with a groan. Rand caught him before he was flat on the ground and dragged him backward, behind a shelf of rock and mostly hidden by a pile of weathered logs that was probably once a miner's cabin. He felt for the man's pulse— strong and steady—then used a bandanna from his pack as a gag and tied him up with rope he also took from his pack.

Harley returned and sniffed at the unconscious man. When the guard was safely silenced and trussed, Rand patted the dog. "I don't know if you meant to distract him and make him walk over, but it worked." He straightened. "Come on. We don't have time to waste. Let's find your mom."

Harley raced ahead to the gate across the opening to the mine and barked. "Chris!" Rand called, keeping his voice low. "Chris, are you in there?"

"Rand? Harley?" Then Chris was standing there—or at least, a woman who sounded like Chris but was dressed in a shapeless gray dress that came almost to her ankles and a blond wig that sat crookedly on her head. "Rand, what are you doing here? Where's the guard?"

"The guard is tied up behind some rocks. And I'm here to get you out."

"There's a lock on the door." This, from a girl who appeared beside Chris—the same girl Rand had seen emerging from the woods on his visit to the camp with the sheriff and his deputy. Serena.

"This is Serena." Chris put a hand on the girl's shoulder.

"We've met before," he said.

"You're the man who tried to help Lana," Serena said. "How are you going to get us out of here? The gate is locked."

Rand moved over to examine the chain and heavy padlock. Then he turned his attention back to Chris. "I'm going to have to shoot the lock off." He drew the pistol once more.

Chris looked alarmed. "Someone will hear you."

"They probably will," he said. "So you have to be prepared to run as soon as I get the gate open."

Chris pulled the wig from her head and tossed it to the ground, then shucked the dress off over her head, revealing the jeans and top she had been wearing yesterday. "I'm ready." She took the girl's hand. "And Serena is coming with us."

Serena pulled free of Chris's grasp. "I'm too slow. I'll hold you back."

"No. I promised I wouldn't leave you. You're coming with us."

"You're coming with us," Rand agreed. He hefted the pistol. "Stand back, then get ready to run."

CHRIS COULD HARDLY believe Rand had found her, but she had no illusions that getting away from Jedediah and the others would be easy. They would have to have luck on their side.

Serena huddled against her. Chris clasped one of the girl's hands tightly and pulled her closer. The child was trembling. "It's going to be okay," Chris whispered.

A deafening blast of gunfire shook the air. Chris flinched and wrapped both arms around Serena. "Come on!" Rand shouted as he dragged open the gate. "Hurry!"

They scrambled out of the cave and up the steep slope to the left, loose rock sliding beneath their feet. Harley bounded ahead of them, leaping from rock to rock like a mountain goat. Chris grabbed hold of clumps of grass to pull herself up, while Serena scrambled on hands and knees ahead of her. "This way," Rand urged.

As they topped the rise, shouts rose behind them. "They're coming!" Serena cried.

"Run!" Rand urged.

They ran, the dog bounding along beside them. Serena cried out and she stumbled and fell. Rand doubled back and scooped her up. He boosted her onto his back, and she clung there, gripping his shoulders, her legs wrapped around his torso. Chris looked forward again and ran.

Though she was in good shape from training for search and rescue, she wasn't a runner. The rocky, uneven ground made it impossible to achieve any kind of regular pace.

Every few feet, she stumbled or planted a foot wrong, and the thin air at this altitude soon had her gasping for breath. She could hear Rand laboring behind her.

She slowed, panting, and looked back the way they had come. "I don't see anyone coming after us," she said.

"Keep moving," he said. "We need to put as much distance between us and them as possible." He led the way, cutting across the top of the ridge, then plunging down a long barren slope. Thunder shook the sky, and fat raindrops began to fall. Chris's feet slid out from under her and she fell, but she scrambled up again, ignoring the pain in her left ankle, and staggered after Rand.

At the bottom of the slope was an area of scrubby trees. They plunged into this cover as the rain began to fall harder, staying closer together. "You can put me down now," Serena said.

Rand lowered her to the ground and straightened. "This way!" He pointed to their right, and they set off at a fast walk.

"Where are we going?" Chris asked.

"Back toward the mill," he said. "There will be searchers and probably law enforcement there."

"Will they help us?" Serena asked.

"Yes," Rand said. "They will help us."

"I'm scared," Serena said.

"I am too," Chris said. "But it's going to be okay."

The trees where they had sought cover thinned, and they emerged on open ground once more.

"Stop right there." Jedediah and two men armed with rifles stepped out to surround them.

SERENA HUDDLED BESIDE CHRIS, her shoulders shaking as she silently wept. Chris rubbed her shoulder. "It's going to be okay," she murmured. Was that the right thing to say or only one more lie to a child who had been raised on lies?

Jedediah moved toward them. Harley put himself between Chris and the men with guns, barking furiously.

Jedediah aimed the rifle at the dog. "No!" Chris shouted, and lunged for the dog's collar. "Harley, no!"

The dog quieted. Chris continued to hold him and glared at Jedediah. "You will have to learn obedience," he said. "The Exalted will make sure you do."

Serena began to weep more loudly. "I didn't want to go with them!" she said. "They made me." She sank to her knees at Jedediah's feet. "Please forgive me! I would never betray the Exalted! He is everything!"

Rand stood a few feet away, a guard on either side of him. They had taken his pistol and his pack. He caught Chris's eye, his expression questioning. She shook her head. Serena had certainly come with them willingly, but now she was terrified, saying what she had to in order to survive.

"Get up," Jedediah ordered.

When Serena didn't move, the fourth man pulled her upright and marched her away. Jedediah moved in beside Chris. She stood. Harley remained between her and Jedediah but kept quiet. "Move," Jedediah said.

They trudged for almost an hour in silence, only the occasional crunch of gravel beneath their feet or labored breathing on a steep slope punctuating their steady pace. A steady downpour soaked their clothing and left them shivering. Thunder rumbled, and jagged lightning forked across the sky. Chris flinched with each mighty crack and wondered at the chances of being struck by one of the bolts.

They descended into a narrow valley and finally stopped beside a metal shipping container set against a large boulder. Jedediah nudged Chris in the ribs with the barrel of the rifle. "Get in," he ordered. "You'll wait here for the helicopter."

Fighting rising panic, Chris moved into the container—a long metal box without windows. Her footsteps rang hollowly, a dull sound beneath the staccato beat of rain on the metal top and sides of the container. Harley trotted in beside her, the tick of his toenails signaling his path across the floor. Rand stumbled in last. As the door swung shut behind them, Chris caught a glimpse of Serena's tear-streaked face as she stared after them.

The door closed, plunging them into darkness. Chris reached out a hand and Rand clasped it, a reassuring anchor in this sea of fear. The sound of a bar being fit over the door, followed by the drag of chains, signaled their imprisonment. She put her free hand over her chest, as if to keep her painfully beating heart from bursting from her skin.

They stood there for a long moment, saying nothing. Gradually, her eyes adjusted and she realized they weren't in total darkness. Light showed around the door and broke through pinpoint holes in the container's metal sides. The container was empty except for a metal pail in the corner, which she assumed was meant to serve as their toilet. Rand released her hand and walked over to the door. He ran his fingers along the gaps around it, then shook his head. "I don't see any way to pry it open."

"I doubt if we'll be here long," Chris said.

Rand returned to your side. "What was that about a helicopter?"

"The Exalted apparently has a helicopter now. He's sending it to pick me up."

"A helicopter won't fly in this storm," Rand said.

"It sounds like the rain is slowing," Chris said. The drops were more intermittent now, and she only had to raise her voice slightly to be heard over their patter.

"What will happen to Serena?" Rand asked.

"I don't know." She clasped Rand's hand again. His warm grasp calmed her. "You know she only said those things because she was frightened," she said. "She was born to the group. She's been told all her life that if she ever leaves them, she'll be condemned for eternity. She's just a child."

"I'm not blaming her," he said. He squeezed her hand. "Was it like that for you? Were you afraid to leave?"

"No. But I wasn't born in the group. And while my father was a true believer—at least for a while—my mother never really was. She went along to be with my father. She said at first it wasn't so bad. She liked the idea of living off the land with a like-minded group of people. But the more time passed, and the more she saw how the Exalted brainwashed people into obedience, the more resistant she was to remaining in the group. I remember she and my dad argued about it." She fell silent, trying to judge if the rain was really slowing. "I won't get on that helicopter with him," she said. "I won't."

He put his arm around her shoulder. "I'll do everything I can to stop him," he said. "For now, all we can do is wait." He sat and she lowered herself to sit beside him. Harley settled on her other side. The metal floor and sides of the container were cold, and she shivered in her damp clothing, her wet hair plastered around her head. She laid her head on Rand's shoulder and closed her eyes. She was still afraid, worried about what Jedediah and the others might do to her, about what would happen if she was taken away with the Exalted, and about where Serena might be right now.

The rain and Rand's warmth must have lulled her to sleep. She started awake at the scrape of the bar over the metal door being lifted and Harley's loud barking. "Harley, hush!" she commanded, and the dog fell silent once more. The door of the container opened wider, enough for someone to be shoved inside, then it clanged shut once more.

Rand was already kneeling beside the crumpled figure on the floor. "Serena, are you okay?" he asked.

Chris joined him, then gasped as Rand gently shifted the girl toward the light. One side of her face was swollen and bruised, and a thin trickle of blood trailed from the corner of her lip. "Did Jedediah do this?" Chris demanded.

Serena nodded and continued to sob.

Chris pulled her close. "It's okay," she murmured. "They had no right to hurt you."

Serena sobbed harder. "I didn't mean it," he said. "Those things I said about you making me go with you. I was scared of Jedediah. I didn't want him to hurt me."

"I know." Chris stroked the girl's back.

"Bad things happen to people who disobey the Exalted," Serena said. "That's why my parents died."

"I told you my mother and I left the Vine when I was about your age," Chris said. "I was scared, like you. But things worked out for us. I make my living as an artist. I have friends and I volunteer to help others. I never could have done any of those things if I had stayed with the Vine."

Serena sniffed and wiped her eyes with her fingers. "But they caught you. They made you come back."

"They won't keep me," Chris said. "And they won't keep you either."

"How are we going to get away?" Serena asked. "There are more guards this time."

"We'll find a way," Chris said. She couldn't afford not to believe that. There was so much more at stake than her own safety. Serena's and Rand's lives were also at stake—two people who were becoming more and more important to her.

Chapter Sixteen

Rand left Chris to deal with Serena and paced the shipping container, his steps ringing on the floor. In the dim light, he examined the sides of the container. "I'm trying to find some weakness we can use to our advantage," he said. After a full circuit of the box, he ended up beside Chris and Serena once more. Serena had stopped crying and was sitting with her arm around Harley, stroking his side.

"Search and rescue and the sheriff's department will still be searching for us," he said. He spoke just loud enough to be heard over the rain but not loud enough for the guards to make out his words.

"Maybe not in this rain," Chris said. "The safety of the searchers always comes first."

"I could try to overpower the guards," he said.

"There are three of them, plus Jedediah," Serena said.

"And they have guns," Chris said. "I think our best opportunity is going to be when they try to move us. Maybe we can create some kind of distraction. I could pretend to faint?" Even to her ears, the plan sounded dubious.

"When they come to get us, they're going to have all three guards and maybe some reinforcements from the camp or the helicopter," Rand said. "That's also likely to be when they decide to deal with me—either right before or right after you leave."

An icy shiver raced through her. "What do you mean, 'deal' with you?" she asked.

"They don't have any intention of sending me with you and Serena in that helicopter," he said. "They'll get me out of the way as soon as possible."

Chris stared. She wanted to protest, but she saw the truth in his words. Jedediah wouldn't want to deal with Harley either. If they were all going to get out of this alive, they had to figure out a way to escape before the helicopter arrived.

"We need to eliminate the guards one at a time," Rand said. He looked toward the door. "It would help if we could see who was out there. I'm guessing the guards take shifts, with only one or two at a time here at the container."

"There's a gap around the door," Serena said. She moved over to the door and pressed her eye to the gap. "From down here I can see out." Pause. "I see two guys. One is sitting on a rock, huddled under a tarp. The other is pacing back and forth. He's wearing a poncho. They both look pretty wet and miserable."

Rand moved closer to Chris. One hand resting on her shoulder, he leaned over and spoke in her ear. "If you can create some kind of distraction, maybe we can get the guards inside and overpower them."

"That will only work if they both come in here," she said.

"They might welcome the chance to get out of the rain. Or, if you can create a big enough ruckus, they might believe they'll need to work together to subdue you."

She nodded. "I'm willing to try."

He looked around. "I wish I had something I could use to hit them over the head. Even a big rock would do."

There were no rocks in the shipping container, and the guards had taken their packs. "There's the slop bucket," she said. "But it's empty."

"It has sand or cat litter in it," he said. "If we throw that in their faces, it will momentarily blind them. Maybe enough for me to get hold of one of their guns."

"That's a lot of *if*s," she said. "But I can't think of a better idea."

RAND WASN'T CONVINCED his plan would work, but he couldn't see a viable alternative. "Serena," he called. "We need your help."

She joined them, and Rand explained their plan. "We need you to stay to one side and keep hold of Harley," Rand said. "As soon as I give the word, you take off running, out of the container and away from the area. Chris and I will be right behind you."

She nodded. "All right." She took hold of the dog's collar and coaxed him to the front corner of the container, just to the right of the door.

Rand looked at Chris. "Are you ready?"

She blew out a breath. "Ready."

He moved to the left of the door and she faced it, then threw back her head and let out a shriek. Rand started. "Oh no, oh no, oh no!" she shouted. "Help! Someone please help!" The hair on the back of his neck rose. If he hadn't known she was faking, he would have been totally convinced.

Someone pounded on the door. "Quiet down in there!" a man yelled.

Chris shrieked even louder. "No! No! Please help! Help!"

"What's going on?" a second male voice demanded.

More shrieks and wails from Chris. Serena joined in.
"Oh no! It's horrible. Help! Help!"

The chain rattled, followed by the scrape of the bar. The
door creaked open, and one man stuck his head inside.
"What's going on in here?"

Chris sank to the floor and thrashed around, moaning
and groaning. The first guard moved inside. Chris thrashed
harder and shrieked more. "You have to help her!" Serena
pleaded.

Harley began barking, adding to the deafening echo
within the container. The first guard knelt beside Chris
and grabbed her arm. She rolled away from him, thrash-
ing harder.

"You need to hold her down, or she'll hurt herself," Serena cried.

"Joel, get in here!" the first guard cried. "I need your
help!"

The second guard stepped inside. "What's going on?"

"Help me with her," the first guard said.

Joel moved in and stood beside the first man.

Rand rushed forward. He hurled the contents of the pail
into the face of first one man and then the other. They staggered, and he punched the first man, breaking his nose.
Then he wrenched the rifle from the guard's hands and
used it as a club to hit the second man. He went down, and
Harley immediately bit him.

"Get him off me!" the first man screamed.

"Harley, release!" Chris shouted. She was on her feet
now. She picked up the second man's rifle and hit him over
the head. Both men were on the ground now—one unconscious, the other groaning.

"Let's go!" Rand grabbed her hand.

"Serena!" Chris called.

"I'm right here. Harley, follow me." She raced out the door, and the others followed.

The rain hit them in an icy downpour. Rand scanned the area but saw no other guards. Maybe the storm had muffled the sounds of their struggle enough that Jedediah and the third guard hadn't heard. "Which way do we go?" Chris asked.

Rand had no idea, but he reasoned Jedediah and the other guard were probably somewhere facing the door of the container. "This way!" He pointed to the rear of their former prison.

They ran, slipping on mud and slick rock but getting up and going again. Serena stayed with them, the dog at her side. Their course gradually took them downhill. Rand tried to picture the topo map of the area he had studied last night, but he couldn't relate this soggy landscape to what had been printed there. All they could do was continue to put distance between themselves and their captors.

After what felt like an hour but was probably only a fraction of that, they entered a drainage, clumps of grass and wildflowers replacing bare rock, a thin trickle of water cutting a path ahead of them. The rain slowed, then stopped, and the sky began to clear. Rand stopped beneath a rock ledge and they rested, waiting for their breathing to return to normal before anyone spoke. "Where are we going?" Serena asked.

"I don't know," Rand admitted. "But a drainage like this should lead to a stream or a road or something." He hoped. He wasn't certain that was true.

Chris looked up the way they had just come. "I don't hear anyone following us," she said.

"Maybe they're gathering reinforcements." He straightened. "Let's keep going."

They walked now, instead of running, but they kept a steady pace. No one complained, though he knew they were all hungry and tired. He fell into step beside Serena. "How are you doing?" he asked. "Are you in pain?"

She shrugged. "My face hurts. But I'll be okay."

The drainage they had been following did end—not at a stream or road but in a box canyon. They spent the next two hours picking their way up the canyon walls, grappling with mud and loose rock before finally emerging at the top as the sun was sinking. "We need to find a place to spend the night," Rand said.

They studied the landscape. Rand wished he had his pack and binoculars. "That looks like a building over there." Chris pointed to the west. "Maybe an old mine ruin."

They trudged in the fading light toward the structure, which proved to be the remains of a cabin, the roof mostly gone and one wall collapsing. But they cleared out a dry spot at the back. With the darkness, the temperature had dropped, and they were all shivering, with no way to make a fire.

"Let's huddle together," Chris said. "We'll keep each other warm."

They put Serena between them, with Harley at her feet. Soon, she was breathing evenly, asleep. Chris stroked her hair. "I'm still so angry that they beat her," she said softly. "She's just a child."

"She's safe with us now," Rand said. But for how much longer? The Exalted and his followers had proved they were relentless in their pursuit.

"Why does he want me so badly?" she asked. "Why go to so much trouble to have me?"

"Maybe it's because you defied him and got away," Rand said. "He wants revenge, or to make an example of you for his followers. Or maybe he's obsessed. He's decided he has to have you, and that's what drives him." He wrapped his arm around her. "But I'm not going to let him have you." He didn't know how he could stop them, but he would do everything in his power to keep her with him.

She tilted her head back and looked up, blinking rapidly. He wondered if she was holding back tears.

"THE WORLD LOOKS so big from here," Rand said.

She nodded. Her world inside the Vine had been so small. Everything revolved around the Exalted and life in the camps. Their whole focus was obeying the Exalted, serving him and, thus, somehow, perfecting themselves. Even though she had told Rand she wasn't as fully indoctrinated as Serena, it had taken her a long time after she and her mother had left to accept that no one and no situation was perfect.

Rand leaned in closer, and she turned toward him. She shifted until she was pressed against him, then kissed him. The kiss was a surrender—not to him as much as to the part of her that wanted to rest, to feel safe in his arms. And it was a release of the tension she had been holding in too long. She had fought against trusting anyone else for so many years that it had become second nature, but Rand made her want to trust him, with her secrets, her fears and her very life. The feeling both frightened and thrilled her, and she did her best to translate those sensations into that kiss.

He brought his hand up to caress the side of her neck, and she leaned into his touch. She wanted to be closer to him, but the child between them prevented that. She had to be content with drinking in the taste of him, the soft pressure of his lips, the firm caress of his hand. She wished she could see more of his face in the darkness, but maybe that only heightened the experience of that kiss. It warmed her through and fed a growing desire within her. "I wish we were alone, somewhere more comfortable," she whispered.

"If I have to be here," he said, "I'm glad it's with you."

She laughed, more nerves than mirth. "You have a strange idea of romance."

He kissed her again. Okay, not strange at all. If he could make her feel this way with a kiss, imagine what he could do with more time and room.

Serena moaned and stirred between them, and they pulled apart a little. Their situation was truly awful— stranded and lost, pursued by people who probably wanted to kill Rand and Harley and make Serena's and Chris's lives miserable. But Chris was no longer afraid. Was this what it was like to be in love?

RAND WOKE BEFORE DAWN, cold and stiff and hungry. He tried to extricate himself from the tangle they had slept in without disturbing the others, but Chris woke up. "Is something wrong?" she asked.

"I'm just getting up to stretch my legs." He stood, wincing as he straightened his aching limbs. "I'm going to see if I can find us some water."

Outside, the damp chill of early morning stung his skin. The sky had lightened from black to sooty gray. Rand picked his way across a stretch of gravel into a clump of willows. Just beyond the willows, a spring seeped from the ground into a moss-rimmed pool. He knelt and scooped water into his hand. It was clear and sweet smelling. He drank deeply, scooping water into his mouth over and over. They would all probably have to be treated for the giardia bacteria that was endemic in mountain waterways, but that was a small price to pay for freedom.

A buzzing startled him and he leaped to his feet, searching for the source of the sound. It came from the sky. He looked up and saw a drone hovering overhead. He immediately crouched and burrowed farther into the cover of the willows. Had the drone seen him? The sheriff's department had a drone they were using to search for Chris. Was this it? Or did it belong to the Vine?

He waited until the drone was out of sight, the sound of its buzzing fading, and hurried back to the miner's shack. Chris and Serena were both up now, and Chris was braiding Serena's long dark hair. "I found a spring," Rand said. "The water is cool and sweet."

"I'm so thirsty," Serena said. She rubbed her stomach. "Hungry too."

"I know." Rand patted her shoulder. "I'm hoping we'll be safe and eating a good dinner by tonight."

"Did you see anything to indicate which way we should go?" Chris asked. She finished the braid and wrapped the end with a strip of what looked like torn T-shirt. Dark shadows beneath her eyes and her pale complexion betrayed her weariness. But she was still the most beautiful woman he knew. The memory of the kisses they had shared last night sent heat through him. He believed she was starting to trust him, and he hoped that would lead to a future together.

She was looking at him curiously, and he realized he hadn't answered her question. "I didn't look around much."

He hesitated, then added, "I spotted a drone. I don't know if it saw me or not."

"What's a drone?" Serena asked.

"It's like a miniature helicopter with a camera attached," Rand said. "It can fly around and take pictures of anything on the ground. Do you know if the Vine has anything like that?"

She shook her head. "I never saw anything like that."

Rand glanced at Chris. "The sheriff said he would be using a drone to search for you. I'm hoping this one belongs to them, but I wasn't sure, so I stayed out of the open."

Chris dusted off her hands. "Let's get a drink and see if we can figure out where to head next."

Rand led the way to the little spring, and they took turns drinking the water. Chris walked along the stream for a short distance, then returned. "I can't tell if it goes anywhere or not."

"Let's climb up a little higher and see if we can find a spot with a better view of the countryside."

They moved slowly up a steep hill behind the ruins of the cabin. Even Serena was moving with little energy today. If they didn't find help soon, they were going to be in real trouble. No food, little water and little sleep were starting to take their toll. At the top, Rand studied the land spread out before them—a cream-and-brown-and-gold expanse of rock, like taffy spilling from the pot. Clumps of trees and falling-down mine ruins and rusted equipment dotted the landscape as if scattered by a child's hand. He fixed his gaze on a narrow band of white cutting across a slope below.

"Is that a road?" Chris asked.

He nodded. "I think so." Probably a backcountry Jeep road, but if they could reach it and head downhill, they would eventually come to a more major road, with traffic and people and the help they needed.

They set off, grateful for the easier downhill travel but at the same time aware of how exposed they were on the treeless slope. He kept glancing overhead, wondering if the drone would return.

As if responding to his thoughts, a distant buzzing reached them. "What's that noise?" Serena asked.

Rand scanned the sky. The drone was flying straight toward them. There was nowhere to hide. He dropped into a squat. "Get down," he said. "If we can blend into the rock, it might not see us." It was a trick used by prey animals—freeze and hope the predator doesn't notice.

They huddled together on the ground as the drone passed over them. It didn't hover or circle back. Was it possible they had avoided detection again?

They hurried on. Rand was anxious to reach the cover of the trees. They were almost there when a much louder sound cut the air—a deep throbbing he felt in his chest. "It's a helicopter!" Serena shouted.

"Run for the trees!" Rand yelled.

Chapter Seventeen

They ran, but the helicopter was gaining fast. They were still a hundred yards from the tree line when the first bullet struck a rock near Rand's feet, sending chips of granite flying. "Spread out!" he shouted. The farther apart they were, the harder it would be for whoever was firing to get them all.

Chris headed off in a sharp diagonal. Serena took off after her. Rand headed in the opposite direction. Another bullet hit a boulder near him. A fragment of rock hit the side of his face. He wiped at it, and his fingers came away bloody. He put his head down and kept running.

He was almost to cover when gunfire ripped from the trees. Yet the bullets weren't aimed at him—but at the helicopter. The chopper rose sharply and veered away. A man in black tactical gear stepped out of the trees, a rifle cradled in his arms. Rand froze.

"Are you all right, Rand?" The man lifted the visor of his helmet, and Rand recognized Deputy Ryker Vernon.

Chris and Serena caught up with them. Serena clung to Chris and stared at Ryker. "We're good now that we're with you," Rand said.

Ryker looked up at the sky. "Do you know who that was, shooting at you?"

"The helicopter belongs to the Vine," Chris said. "Their

leader, Edmund Harrison, was probably in there with some of his followers."

"They kidnapped Chris and Serena and were going to take them away from here in a helicopter," Rand said. "The storm yesterday delayed them, and we managed to get away."

"I'm still nervous, out in the open like this," Chris said. "Can we please leave?"

"There's a group coming up to help us," Ryker said.

Rand heard voices approaching. Soon, two deputies and half a dozen search and rescue members joined them. "Is everybody okay?" Danny asked.

"We're good," Chris said.

"Rand, you're bleeding." Hannah studied his face.

Rand swiped at his cheek. "A rock chip hit me. I'll be okay. You can clean it up later. Right now I just want to leave."

"Who is this?" Danny addressed Chris, but he was looking at Serena.

"This is Serena." Chris kept her hand on the girl's shoulder.

"What's your last name, Serena?" Bethany asked.

"It's Rogers." Serena looked up at Chris. "I'd almost forgotten that."

Chris nodded. "Members of the Vine don't use last names," she explained to the others.

"Chris!"

She looked up to see Bethany hurrying toward her. The younger woman threw her arms around Chris and hugged her, hard. After a second's hesitation, Chris returned the hug. It felt good. "I'm so glad to see you!" Bethany said. "I've been so worried." Her voice broke.

"Hey, it's okay." Chris patted her shoulder. "I'm good."

Bethany released her hold and wiped her eyes. "I'm glad to hear it. I'd hate to think I'd lost a new friend."

"Yeah. I'd hate that too," Chris said. She meant it. "Let's get together for lunch again soon."

"Let's. I can fill you in on my family's latest plan for taking over my life." Bethany laughed and turned away.

"We have some vehicles waiting at the road to take you back to Eagle Mountain," Jake said.

"Do you have any food?" Serena asked. "We're starving."

This prompted the rescuers to dig into their packs and produce an assortment of nuts, dried fruit, protein bars, chocolate and gummy candy. Chris, Serena and Rand gratefully accepted this bounty. Danny examined Serena's bruises and treated her busted lip. They ate as they walked, a new vigor in their step. Rand glanced ahead toward Chris, who was chatting with Bethany. They were safe, for now. But could he continue to protect her from the Vine, as long as they were still free?

"WHAT WILL HAPPEN to Edmund Harrison and the rest of his followers?" Chris addressed this question to Sheriff Walker as soon as he entered the interview room at the sheriff's department, where she and Rand were seated, only a few hours after their rescue.

"We have a BOLO out for his arrest," Travis said. "And we're continuing to search for the rest of the group."

"Where is Serena?" Chris asked. "You can't let her go back to those people. You saw the bruises on her, right?"

"She's with Deputy Jamie Douglas right now," Travis said. "We've summoned a child-welfare advocate. They're working on finding an emergency placement for her."

"She can stay with me," Chris said. She leaned forward, hands clenched in her lap. "She trusts me, and I understand some of what she's been through."

"You'll have to take that up with the child-welfare person," Travis said. He settled into the chair across from them. "What I need from you is everything you know about the people who kidnapped you."

The last thing Chris wanted was to sit there and give them all the details about the Vine. But she pushed aside her annoyance and told Travis what she knew, about the group's history, its habits and the people involved in the group now. She and Rand described the various guards and the woman they had seen with Jedediah. "Jedediah is the one you really need to find," she said. "He's the Exalted's right-hand man."

"The Exalted is what they call Edmund Harrison?" Travis verified.

"Yes. And he's got most of them so brainwashed they'll do anything he says."

"And you indicated they're armed?"

"I saw at least three rifles," Rand said. "And one of them took my pistol."

"I never saw firearms when I was with the group," Chris said. "But that was fifteen years ago. And they never shied away from violence against their own members, though they called it 'punishment.'"

"We'll talk to Serena once the child advocate is with her," Travis said. "She may be able to tell us more, including where the group might be now."

"They're very skilled at packing up and vanishing in the middle of the night," Chris said. "They did it often when I was living with them. They talked about moving on to enlighten a new audience of people who could benefit from their message, but later I decided they probably left to avoid too much attention from local law enforcement."

Travis nodded, then stood. "You two are free to go. We'll be in touch."

"I think Chris—and maybe Serena too—are still in danger," Rand said. "The Exalted has gone to a lot of trouble to pursue them. I'm not sure he'll give up so easily."

"Do you want us to find a shelter for you to stay in?" Travis asked.

"No." She looked at Rand but said nothing. If the Vine tracked her to his place, she would be endangering him also. "But maybe I should go somewhere like that."

"You can stay with me." Rand took her hand. "But it wouldn't hurt to have a deputy cruise by occasionally."

"We're spread thin as it is, searching for all these people," Travis said. "But I'll do what I can."

Harley was waiting for them in the lobby. Someone had fed and watered the dog, and he looked none the worse for the ordeal of the last forty-eight hours. Chris wished she could say the same. She was exhausted, as well as worried about Serena and about the Exalted. Those moments when that helicopter had hovered over them, bullets ricocheting off the rocks, had been among the most terrifying of her life.

Back at Rand's house, he insisted on checking everything before she and Harley went in. She spent several anxious moments on his front porch, waiting until he returned. "Nothing's disturbed," he said. "You can come in now."

They filed inside. The house was quiet, nothing out of place. She told herself she could relax, but tension still pulled at her shoulders. "You can have the shower first," he told her.

"Can I have a bath?" she asked. "I'd really like to soak in a tub."

"Sure. There's a tub in the primary bath. Let me get my things, and I'll shower in the guest room while you soak."

"Thanks," she said, too weary to make even a polite token protest about him giving up his bathroom for her.

She went to the guest room and dug out clean clothes and her toiletries. Rand still hadn't appeared by the time she returned to the hall outside his room. She heard running water. Had he decided to take a shower first after all?

She was about to knock and check on him when he finally came out of his bedroom. "I was just getting everything ready for you," he said.

She followed him back into the primary bedroom, past the king-size bed with its blue duvet neatly pulled over the pillows. He opened the bathroom door to a fog of steam and gestured toward a garden tub, already filled, froths of bubbles floating on the top. He had arranged candles along the far edge of the tub and lit them, and the scents of lavender and vanilla made a soothing cloud around them.

Tears stung her eyes. "You didn't have to go to so much trouble."

"You're worth any amount of effort," he said, and took her in his arms.

They kissed, a heady caress that left her dizzy and breathless. Rand slid his hand beneath her shirt and rested it at her waist. "I should let you bathe in peace," he said.

She moved in even closer. "I think that tub is big enough for two."

He didn't protest, but pushed her shirt up farther. She

helped him guide it over her head, then reached back to un-snap her bra. His hands were hot on her breasts, his fingers gentle but deft as he stroked and teased her. She stripped off the rest of her clothing with shaking hands, clinging to him for balance but also because she wanted to be closer to him.

He was naked in no time, and her breath caught at the sight of him. It had been a long time since she had been this excited about a man, and she was both eager and anxious. When he stepped into the tub, she followed, the silky, warm bubbles closing over them. She let out a sigh as she sank beneath the water, then lay back, her head on a folded towel, and closed her eyes.

The water sloshed as Rand shifted, and then something soft and slightly ticklish glided over her body. She started to open her eyes and sit up. "Relax," he said. "Keep your eyes closed. Enjoy your bath."

She decided the soft and ticklish thing was a soapy sponge he was using to caress first her shoulders, then her breasts. The sponge coasted across her stomach and stroked her thighs, then traveled down her legs to her foot and her toes. She suppressed a giggle as Rand soaped each digit, then slid his hand up the back of her leg, gently massaging. He did the same to the other leg. His touch was gentle but firm, enjoyable but not exactly relaxing.

She wasn't sure when he replaced the sponge with his hands, but she realized it had happened when he began stroking between her thighs, caressing her sex, stoking the passion that began to build.

A moan escaped her, and she opened her eyes and stared at him. His eyes locked on hers, the heat in his expression scorching. "Do you want me to stop?" he asked.

"No." Her answer came out barely audible. She cleared

her throat. "No." But even as he continued to tease her, she straightened and wrapped her hand around his erection.

His reaction was immediate and gratifying—a widening of his eyes and a renewed alertness. His hand stilled as she began to stroke him. "Do you want me to stop?" she teased.

"No." But his hand moved from between her legs to her shoulders. He pulled her forward until she was resting on top of them, water sloshing over the edge of the tub as she moved.

"The floor's getting wet," she said.

"That's not the only thing," he said as he slid two fingers inside her.

There she went, giggling again. Definitely not like her. But being with Rand did that—made her feel like someone else. Someone freer and happier than she had ever been.

They kissed again, hands exploring, caressing, teasing as their lips tasted and nipped and murmured appreciation. "That feels so good."

"You're so beautiful."

"Whatever you do, don't stop."

A second tidal wave of water sloshed over when she moved to crouch over him. "Maybe it's time to take this to the bed," she said.

"Good idea."

They helped each other out of the tub; then he insisted on toweling her off, the plush but slightly rough surface of the towel gliding over sensitive nerve endings, ramping up her arousal. He paused to suck first one nipple, then another, a delicious torture that had her squirming.

At last he raised his head, grinning. She realized he had taken the time to shave, the stubble that had grown in the past two days erased, replaced by smooth skin. "Let me get a condom," he said, and opened a drawer beside the sink.

His bedroom was dark and cool, the bed soft, the scent of lavender and vanilla drifting out with the steam from the bathroom. But she only noted these details in passing. Her focus was on him as he lay beside her and pulled her into his arms. They stared into each other's eyes. She didn't let herself look away, as she might have done before. Whatever there was to see in her, she wanted him to see it.

"Why did you come looking for me?" she asked. "By yourself, I mean, instead of part of the official search."

"I thought I knew where to find you, and I didn't want to wait on the others."

"But why look at all?" she asked. "I'm not your responsibility."

"Because I love you," he said.

She flinched at the words. She tried to hide her reaction, but he couldn't miss it. "Does that scare you, when I say it out loud?" he asked.

"A little," she admitted.

"You're strong enough to face your fear," he said.

"Yes, I am." But the wonderful thing about being with Rand was that she didn't have to be strong. She didn't have to fight or resist or do anything. She could relax and surrender without giving up anything.

So she did. She smiled and closed her eyes. She allowed him to touch her in all the ways that felt good, and she did the same for him, until they came together with urgency and need. She gave herself up to the building passion and the incredible release that followed.

Afterward, she lay curled in his arms, tears sliding down her cheeks. "Why are you crying?" he asked.

"I don't know," she admitted. "But it feels good." She hadn't allowed herself many tears over the years, afraid they made her look weak. Rand had taught her to see things differently. Feeling wasn't a weakness, and being vulnerable wasn't wrong. She would have to practice to fully believe those things, but she was willing to make the effort.

THEY HAD BEEN asleep for a while when Rand woke to Harley's frantic barking. "What is it?" Chris asked.

"I don't know." He got out of bed and put on his pants and shoved his feet into his shoes. "I'll check."

Harley ran ahead of him down the hall and began barking again—angry, staccato barks like shouts. "No!" someone commanded.

Rand switched on the living room light and found Harley cowering submissively at a man's feet. The man was fit and trim, with stylishly cut silver hair and a tan. He wore a light gray suit with a white shirt and no tie, like a well-off businessman relaxing after work. The man looked from the dog to Rand. "Even dogs know to obey me," he said.

"Who are you?" Rand demanded.

"I'm the Exalted." He smiled a smug grin.

"Edmund Harrison," Rand said.

"That person hasn't existed for years," he said. "I'm the Exalted. And I'm here for Elita. Or, as you know her, Chris. Hand her over and there won't be any trouble."

Rand pressed his back to the wall and surveyed the room.

"Oh, don't worry," Harrison said. "I came alone. The sheriff arrested Jedediah and the rest of my inner circle this afternoon. But I don't need them. All I need is Elita. With her, I'll start a new band of followers."

"How did you find us?" Rand asked.

"Did you forget we have your phone? There's a lot of information on a person's cell phone. I had your address within minutes of my people handing it over to me."

The hallway floor creaked. Rand forced himself not to look back, his eyes fixed on Harrison. The man was walking around the room, studying the books on a shelf. He didn't register that he had heard the noise, though Harley had turned his head that way.

"Harley, come here." Rand snapped his fingers at the dog, who obediently trotted over.

Harrison stopped and looked at Rand. "I'm waiting," he said. "Bring Elita to me, and I'll leave you alone."

"I'm not going to hand Chris over to you," Rand said.

"Then you leave me no choice." Harrison withdrew a pistol from the jacket of his suit. Rand recognized his own gun—the one Jedediah had taken from him. Harrison raised the weapon and aimed it at Rand. "You don't have to worry," he said. "I'm a very good shot. You'll die quickly."

"No!" Chris burst into the room, something in her outstretched hand. When she aimed the item at Harrison, Rand realized it was the wasp spray he had left on the kitchen counter. She squeezed the trigger, and the spray arced across the room, striking Harrison in the face.

Harrison screamed, and the pistol fired twice, striking the floor and the wall. He bent double, clawing at his eyes and coughing. Then Rand was on top of him, wrestling the gun free. Chris dropped the can of insect killer and began kicking at the man who writhed on the floor. Then Harley moved in and began tearing at his arm.

"Stop!" Harrison cried. "He's going to kill me."

"Harley, release!" Chris shouted.

The dog let go, and Rand grabbed the man's bleeding arm and brought it behind his back. "Get me something to tie him with," he said.

Chris left and returned seconds later, tearing at a pillowcase. She handed a strip of fabric to Rand and he used it to bind first Harrison's hands, then his feet. Meanwhile, Chris called 911.

By the time the sheriff arrived, Rand had retrieved his first aid kit and bandaged Harrison's arm. The man hadn't shut up the whole time. He had variously cursed Rand, condemned him to perdition, prophesied a disastrous future for him and railed against the injustice of someone like him being treated this way. "You have no right," Harrison yelled. "This man attacked me without provocation. I want to talk to my lawyer."

"You'll be given a chance to contact your attorney," Travis said. "Meanwhile, anything you say may be used against you in a court of law." He recited the rest of the Miranda rights, even as Harrison continued to rant.

"This is unforgivable," he said. "Why are you arresting me?"

"We'll start with kidnapping, child molestation, theft and murder."

"Murder?" Chris asked.

"We found the bodies of the two young men who brought Danny and Rand into the camp," Travis said.

"I'm innocent," Harrison protested. "This is an outrage." He was still ranting as Dwight and Ryker led him away.

Travis turned to Chris and Rand. "We'll need your statement as soon as you can come to the station," he said.

"He said something about Jedediah being arrested?" Rand asked.

"Yes. We have him and several others in custody. We'll need you to identify the people involved in your kidnapping."

"What about the others?" Chris asked. "The rank and file members of the Vine?"

"We believe we've identified most of them. We're running background checks on all of them, which will take some time. The state is involved, seeing to the welfare of the children in the group. A few people have already been cleared and released. Social services will work to find shelter and assistance for those who might need them."

"Where is Serena?" Chris asked. "When can I see her?"

Travis slipped a card from his pocket. "Here's the number for her caseworker. I told her to expect a call from you."

He said goodbye and left. Chris sank onto the sofa. Rand sat beside her. "I guess it's over," she said.

"We still need to give our statements, and we might have to testify at a trial."

"I meant the Vine. Without the Exalted and his cronies, the group is dead."

Rand took her hand. "How do you feel about that?"

"Relieved," she said. "And…sad. I mean, it could have been something good, but it was just a waste." She looked at him. "I want to do something to help them. Some of those families gave everything they had to the group. Now they'll have nothing."

"We'll see if there are ways we can help them," Rand agreed.

"And I want…" She hesitated, then blurted out, "I want to adopt Serena. I'll contact the state and see what's involved, but I really want to do it."

"You'll make a great mom," he said. He had difficulty getting the words past the sudden lump in his throat.

"Will you help me?" she asked.

"Of course." He squeezed her hand. "I love you."

"I... I love you too," she said.

He kissed her—a gentle caress to seal those words of love. "We're going to figure this out," he said.

"What exactly do you mean?"

"We're going to figure out how to love each other and make it work. How to build a life where you don't have to be afraid of the Vine coming to get you. And we're going to help Serena. Did I leave anything out?"

"I don't think so." They kissed again, and then she rested her head on his shoulder. "You make me believe in things that used to seem impossible. And I mean that in a good way."

"I believe in you. And in us. That's the only thing that matters."

"It is, isn't it?"

Epilogue

Party this way! Posterboard signs directed guests to a gazebo in the town park, which was festooned with helium balloons and crepe paper streamers. Chris stood on the top step of the gazebo and waved to Danny Irwin, Carrie Andrews, and Jake and Hannah Gwynn as they arrived, Carrie's son and daughter in tow. They joined the crowd, which included most of their fellow search and rescue members and all the friends who had made the day possible.

Chris's mom, April, came to stand beside her. "I've got the cake safely stowed in the cooler in the ballfield concession stand," she said. "I'll get a couple of guys to help me bring it over here when it's time."

"Thanks, Mom." April wore a sundress in a pink-rose print, another rose tucked into her pinned-up hair. Her eyes were shining, and she looked younger than her fifty years. "It's so good having you here with us," Chris said.

"It's good to be here."

Danny and Carrie mounted the steps, a large wrapped gift in Danny's hand. Serena skipped up the steps behind them. "Is that present for me?" she asked. In the months since she had come to live with first Chris, then Chris and Rand, she had blossomed into a smart, sensitive child with a deep affection for animals and a love of learning. She had also experienced a growth spurt, necessitating a whole new wardrobe, including the tie-dyed sundress "with the twirly skirt" that she was wearing now. The three of them were in counseling to deal with the trauma she had endured. Chris was surprised by how much the regular meetings with a therapist had helped her deal with her own struggles with her past.

"That depends," Danny said. "Who is this party for?"

"It's for me!" Serena threw her hands into the air.

Danny laughed. "Of course. How could I forget!" He handed over the gift. "Then this is for you."

"Don't mind him." Carrie nudged him. "Happy birthday, Serena."

"Happy birthday!" those around them chorused.

"Do you want to open your gifts before or after the cake?" Chris asked.

"After." She grinned. "It makes it more exciting to wait." She added the package to the pile of gifts on a table in the center of the gazebo, then came over to wrap one arm around Chris and lean against her. "I already got my favorite present."

"You mean, the bicycle?" Rand joined them.

"No. I mean you and Mom."

Chris's heart still struck an extra beat at that word—Mom. It had been a long process through the foster care system to get to this day, but the struggle had been worth it for this precious girl—her daughter.

"And I thought that was the best present *we* ever received," Rand said. He kissed Serena's cheek. She grinned, then caught sight of someone across the yard. "Amber!" she shouted, and ran to catch up with Carrie's daughter.

"Is the adoption final already?" Hannah asked.

"We have a few more months to wait," Chris said. "But there haven't been any setbacks so far." She held up crossed fingers.

"And no more noise from Edmund Harrison and his followers?" Danny asked.

"Harrison is facing more than a dozen charges," Jake said. "He'll go to prison for a long time."

Bethany bounded up the steps to join them. She had made an attempt to confine her brown curls in a bun, but they were already escaping to form a halo around her face. "My dad wants to know when to fire up the grill," she said.

"Tell him any time he's ready," Chris said.

"I'll go tell him," Danny said. "See if he wants some help."

"He's already put my brothers to work," Bethany said. She turned to April. "How are you enjoying your visit to Eagle Mountain, Mrs. Mercer?" she asked.

"Please, call me April. And I'm enjoying it very much. So much I'm thinking of staying. With the Vine uprooted and the Exalted behind bars, it's safe for me to live near my daughter without fear of drawing the wrong sort of attention to her. And I want to get to know my new granddaughter better." She looked over to where Serena stood, surrounded by a trio of girls her age.

"We have something else to celebrate today," Bethany said. She nudged Chris.

Smiling, Chris held out her left hand, sun glinting on the sapphire on the third finger. "We do."

"Congratulations!" Carrie and Hannah chorused, then leaned in for a closer look at the ring.

"Rand, you finally worked up the nerve to propose?" Jake said.

"I asked her months ago," Rand said. "It just took her a while to decide to have me."

Chris blushed. "I wanted to be sure."

He pulled her close. "You were worth waiting for."

Bethany sighed. "If I didn't like you two so much, I'd be jealous. Well, okay, I am a little jealous. But I'm thrilled for you too."

Chris looked down at the ring on her hand. "Everything okay?" Rand whispered.

She nodded. "It's just…overwhelming at times. I have so much—friends, my mom, and you and Serena. All things I thought were out of reach for me."

"I thought they were out of reach for me too," he said. "I used to think the fine details were what made a difference in life. Those were the things that were small enough for me to control. Now I can appreciate the big things—it doesn't get much bigger than having a family and raising a child."

Her eyes met his. The thrill of seeing her love reflected back to her never faded. "We're going to do this," she said. "We are." They kissed, and she was only dimly aware of the cheering around her.

* * * * *

If you missed the previous books in Cindi Myers's
Eagle Mountain: Criminal History miniseries,
you can find them now, wherever
Harlequin Intrigue books are sold!

Mile High Mystery
Colorado Kidnapping
Twin Jeopardy